Missouri Challenge
Finding Home Series

"Daisy"

Verna Clay

For those faced with overwhelming challenges.

*To my Aunt Peggy,
I tried to make this story more adventurous than historical!
Love, Verna Clay*

Missouri Challenge
Finding Home Series
"Daisy"

Copyright © 2013 by Verna Clay

All rights reserved, including the right to reproduce this book or portions thereof in any form whatsoever.

For information contact:
VernaClay@VernaClay.com
Website: www.VernaClay.com

Publisher:
M.O.I. Publishing
"Mirrors of Imagination"

Cover Design:
Verna Clay

Pictures:
CanStockPhoto (Alexis84): Female
CanStockPhoto (SNR): Cabin

This book is a work of fiction. Names, characters, places, and incidents either are products of the author's imagination or are used fictitiously. Any resemblance to actual events or locales or persons, living or dead, is entirely coincidental.

Dear Readers,

Before I started writing this third book in the *Finding Home Series,* I wasn't sure whether to title it after Missouri or Texas because both states (and two romances) are equally divided in the storyline. I chose the name *Missouri Challenge* for a couple of reasons: first, it's the state that Tim Wells and Daisy Smithson's adventure begins in, and second...well, I think I'll let the story reveal that.

Originally, this was meant to be only Daisy and Tim's romance, but in *Rescue on the Rio: Lilah,* I introduced Trent Garrett, the brother of Rush Garrett, and he became such a tortured hero, I just had to find the perfect woman for him. I had a little help when Pearl, the housekeeper of Big G Ranch, whispered in my ear that the heroine for Trent's story was right in his own back yard, so to speak. And after listening to Arizona Cayson's yearning for Trent, I couldn't agree more.

I suppose another reason for naming this book *Missouri Challenge* is because it was so challenging to write. Of course, it could just as easily have been titled *Texas Challenge.*

Enjoy the Challenge,

Verna Clay

Table of Contents

Prologue

Chapter 1: Alcove Spring 1

Chapter 2: Daisy 5

Chapter 3: Renewed Acquaintance 8

Chapter 4: Fixin' What's Broken 15

Chapter 5: Meet the Father 19

Chapter 6: Unexpected News 26

Chapter 7: Plan A 34

Chapter 8: Surprise 38

Chapter 9: Plan B 46

PART TWO: BIG G RANCH
Chapter 10: Banter 56

Chapter 11: Arrival 65

Chapter 12: Bungling No More 71

Chapter 13: Learning from the Best 79

Chapter 14: Helluva Hoedown 83

Chapter 15: Overnight 94

Chapter 16: Morning Walk 99

Chapter 17: Weak Eyes 109

Chapter 18: Mexican Territory 113

Chapter 19: Brand 122

Chapter 20: Tracking Clues 126

Chapter 21: Maria 132

Chapter 22: Brave Women 139

Chapter 23: Return to Sanity 145

Chapter 24: Decisions 149

Chapter 25: Fatted Calf 151

Chapter 26: Trent Confesses 157

Chapter 27: Window to the Soul 163

Chapter 28: Pins and Pa 172

Chapter 29: Encountering the Past 176

Chapter 30: Crooked Tie 187

Epilogue 195

Research Materials for Daisy: Missouri Challenge 196

Author's Note 197

Abby: Mail Order Bride (Excerpt)
Unconventional Series 199

Broken Angel (Excerpt)
Unconventional Series 205

Ryder's Salvation (Excerpt)
Unconventional Series 208

Prologue

May, 1883

Tim Wells bent to kiss Maddie, his fifteen year old sister goodbye, and then patted the head of his ten year old brother, Beau. Next, he hugged his mother tightly and planted a kiss on her cheek. "Don't cry, Ma."

"These are tears of happiness, Tim. In my heart, I know this is a journey you must make."

Tim shook the hand of his stepfather, Cooper Jerome, who pulled him into a tight hug. "We're going to miss you, son."

Having never been away from his family for more than a week or two, Tim was excited, yet sad, to leave. However, before he settled down and started his own family—something he'd been considering over the past year—he needed to return to Missouri and the home he'd known before his father died.

The Oregon Trail had brought him to his new home in Oregon City, but the past was calling. He didn't understand the constant tug on his heart, but he knew if he ignored the call, he would always regret it.

Mounting his horse, he said to no one in particular, "I hope to return before Jake's back from visiting his family in Texas." Jake was Cooper's son from a previous marriage and one of Tim's best friends. His other best friend was Sam Hankerson, a boy he'd befriended while traveling to Oregon in 1866.

His stepfather nodded and Tim could see that he was struggling against strong emotions as he placed his arm around Tim's mother and pulled her against his side.

His ma sniffed and swiped her tears. "You be careful, son."

When his brother and sister also started wiping their eyes, he decided he'd best leave before they were all bawling like babies.

"I love ya'll. Be back soon." He turned his gelding toward the road and urged him into a trot.

Chapter 1: Alcove Spring

After two months of riding the same trail he had traversed seventeen years earlier with his mother and Cooper Jerome, who would later become his beloved step-father, Tim halted Amigo, the horse his parents had given him when he graduated from the small school in Oregon City. He'd been eighteen that year and his friend, Sam Hankerson, as smart as a whip, had graduated with him at the age of fifteen and gone on to higher education in Portland. Sam returned three years later to teach school in Oregon City. By the time his friend was twenty, he was married to Polly, a sweet girl who had lost her parents on the Oregon Trail and been taken in by the Prudence Pittance Orphanage. Sam and Polly were expecting their first child and would be parents when Tim arrived back home. That knowledge boggled Tim's mind.

He resettled his hat against the sun. At one time, he had harbored a secret crush on Polly, but she'd always had eyes for Sam. Since the age of eighteen, there had been a few other girls that caught his attention, but none that made him want to settle down, except maybe Janie Iverson. But that was something he would think about when he returned to Oregon.

In this modern era going from the eastern states to Oregon was accomplished by rail. But now, gazing around the trail, it was as if he had traveled backward in time. Parts of the original trail had been laid with tracks, but other parts seemed not to have changed since Tim's journey all those years ago.

He nudged Amigo forward. He was anxious to reach Alcove Spring and see if he could find their names that Cooper had etched into stone amongst the hundreds already there. An hour later he paused beside a wooden sign painted with faded lettering—ALCOVE SPRING—and smiled. He turned Amigo in the direction of the arrow.

Before he saw the spring, the sound of bubbling water made him feel like a kid again and put a lump in his throat. His mother often said he was like his father, deeply caring and affected by things that other men never gave a passing thought to. He supposed she was right. All his life he had been an observer. He loved animals and plants and trees and mountains and the mists during early morning. He had even penned a few poems that he kept hidden.

He rounded some bushes and came within sight of the spring. Words to one of his poems sprang to mind.

Days dawn
Rivers flow
Time continues evermore
Life is but a dawning and a flowing
Awaiting another sojourner when I cease

Tim smiled at his lapse into sentimentality, but his expression stayed contemplative as he realized the truth of his poem. He watched water cascade off a high ledge into the same basin he remembered from his youth.

Someday my life will cease. What legacy will I leave or will I even be remembered?

He dismounted and circled the basin, reading names and dates that went back as far as the 1840s. He scanned the rocks in search of their names. After a few minutes he found the etchings written one above the other. Aloud, he read, "Tim Wells, Hallie Wells, Cooper Jerome."

Closing his eyes, he could still hear his mother's words. "Just think, all these people have paved the Westward Trails for us. And now, we're paving the way for those after us."

Although Tim felt things deeply, rarely was he moved to tears, but now, remembering that glorious day, he felt close to crying. Walking to their names, he smoothed his hand over the letters. Afterward, he knelt and splashed his face. The water was just as cold as he remembered.

Because he wasn't ready to leave, he sat cross-legged at the water's edge and closed his eyes, thinking of his birth father, Thomas Henry Wells. The tears that had not fallen before now did so. He had loved his kind and generous father. When word of his pa's death in a tornado had reached him and his ma, part of Tim had died that day. For a long time he'd blamed God for allowing his father to travel to St. Louis on the same day as a tornado. The trip had been for the purpose of purchasing tickets for the steamer that would take them from St. Louis to Westport Landing a month later.

Since his father's death, however, Tim had reconciled himself to the fact that perhaps his pa's heroic deed of shielding a little girl from flying debris and saving her life had been for a higher purpose. *One life given so another can live.*

Deep in memories, he absorbed the sounds of water, wind, birds, and remembered good times with his father. Finally, he was ready to leave and finish his journey. His next significant stop would be the home he had lived in with his pa—a home with precious memories that called to him year after year. What would he find there?

Chapter 2: Daisy

At the back of the house, Daisy Smithson hung the laundry she'd just washed, and swiped sweat from her brow. The day was warm and humid, and she berated herself for not starting her chores earlier. Although she disliked washing clothes, she enjoyed hanging them out. She loved feeling the sun and wind on her face and refused to wear a bonnet while pinning clothes on the line.

She reached to hang one of June's diapers and smiled. Her mother's petticoats had been perfect for cutting into squares for that purpose. Glancing at the wooden box under the overhang of the cabin with her two month old daughter wrapped and sleeping inside, her smile widened. Never had she imagined the love she would feel for her tiny bundle. Throughout the dark days of her pregnancy and her shunning by society, she had often felt such despair she'd wished her life would end. Of course, she hadn't known then that June would ease the loneliness of her life and give her a reason to live.

Since the death of her mother three years previous to a stroke, and then her father's death a few months later when his buckboard toppled in the rain and crushed him beneath it, Daisy had not only been left with the running of their small farm, but become the victim of heart wrenching sorrow. As an only child, her father and mother had doted on her with such love she had always felt safe. After their deaths, lonely nights and backbreaking work had taken its toll in physical and mental exhaustion, exacting its greatest damage in emotional upheaval and despair.

Although the townspeople had helped whenever possible with her harvest that first year, and she'd even shown a profit, they had encouraged her to marry, insisting that a woman alone could not run a farm. Something in Daisy had resisted their advice and when men started calling, wanting to court her, she'd felt repulsed by most of them. The vast majority were widowers seeking a mother for their children; a woman to run their households; and a body to warm their beds. Daisy had shunned all their efforts and been chastised by the same townspeople who had once banded together to help her only a year earlier. Eventually, their assistance with planting and harvesting had ceased and she was left to her own devices. She had even become the topic of a sermon by the pastor. Of course, he had not spoken her name, but everyone knew that the rebellious woman disdaining the kindness offered by eligible men of the community to lift her heavy burden was none other than Daisy Smithson.

After that humiliation, Daisy had refused to return to church and had become an outcast from "good" society, as one upstanding woman loudly proclaimed inside the general store while it was packed with customers.

The final undoing of her reputation and severing of contact by that "good" society had been her pregnancy.

As an unmarried woman, she was now the pariah of the community.

Daisy placed a clothespin on the last of her laundry, gazed lovingly at June, and sighed. *I can't bring our crop in alone, baby girl. We might have to travel to the next county to hire hands at harvest time.* She would have to sell her mother's wedding ring to raise funds to pay for help.

A noise from the front of the house alerted her to someone's approach and she ran like a gazelle to lift the box with her baby. Entering the cabin through a back door, she hid June under her bed and rushed to retrieve her rifle. She kept it loaded to discourage unwanted visitors.

Peeking out the curtain of her front window, she watched the approach of a young man on a magnificent steed. Although his face was shadowed and only a smattering of blond hair shown from beneath the wide brim of his hat, something about him seemed familiar. He appeared friendly, but Daisy had no intention of finding out just how friendly. She'd made that mistake once, and although June was the beautiful outcome, she had no inclination to repeat history.

Chapter 3: Renewed Acquaintance

Tim paused on the packed-dirt clearing around the cabin. He'd seen the curtain move and waited for someone to step outside. He frowned at the shabbiness and neglect around him. If he remembered correctly, Mr. and Mrs. Smithson had been meticulous in their care of the home they'd purchased from his parents. Perhaps ownership had changed. After all, it had been seventeen years since he'd left the area.

Even as he glanced around the poorly cared for grounds, nostalgia made him weak. He remembered his father and mother sitting on the porch in the evenings discussing the day's happenings. The old swing on the white oak remained, its wooden seat almost completely decayed. He looked toward the barn and outbuildings where he'd often run errands because of his pa's inability to walk long distances, having suffered infantile paralysis.

The sound of the front door opening brought him back to the present. A small woman with unruly dark red hair stepped onto the porch. She pointed a shotgun at him.

"Mister, you can just turn your horse around and get off my property. I don't cotton to strangers. In fact, I flat out don't like them. As you can see, I got nothin' here worth stealing, so it's best if you leave. That way, I don't have to shoot you."

Tim remembered Daisy's fiery red hair. "Daisy, is that you?"

The slight lowering of the rifle was the only movement the woman made. She didn't respond, but it was enough for Tim to realize this was, indeed, Daisy.

He said, "It's me, Tim Wells. You knew me as Timmy. Maybe you don't remember me, but my pa and ma sold your family this farm when we were eight years old."

Tim watched Daisy's eyes widened, but she didn't lower the gun any more. Instead, she asked bluntly, "Why are you here?"

Tim made an expansive motion with his hands and she tightened her grip on the rifle. He frowned. "I guess you could say I'm revisiting my past. My ma made a new life for us in Oregon, but I've always known one day I would return to my beginnings in Missouri, if only to say a final farewell." He smiled. "Would you mind pointing that gun another direction?"

* * *

Daisy frowned. Timmy Wells? That was Timmy Wells standing in her yard?

She lowered the gun a little. "How do I know you're who you say you are? Last time I saw you we were kids on the back of my pa's buckboard."

The man slowly dismounted and Daisy lifted her gun back up. He noticed and quirked an eyebrow. "Do you remember the dream you told me about?"

The gun went slack in Daisy's hands. "Well, I guess you must be Timmy because I never told anyone else that dream and I'm figuring it wasn't somethin' an eight year old boy would want to spout out."

Timmy grinned and made a waving motion around the yard. "Looks like you're having hard times."

Daisy replied with a hint of humor, "Can't imagine why you'd think that?"

Timmy returned his gaze to her face and held her eyes with his own. "Are your ma and pa still living?"

"No. How 'bout your ma?"

"Yes. She married the man that led us to Oregon and I have a brother, sister, and step-brother."

Daisy smiled. She said, "I'm happy to hear that." She paused and the smile left her face. "My ma died a few years back and my pa not long after." With her free hand she made a waving motion encompassing the farm. "I do the best I can."

"You live here alone?" Timmy asked with a hint of censor.

Daisy bristled. "I do. I've been taking care of myself since my parents died. Me and–" She stopped speaking when the high-pitched squall of her baby pierced the air. Although muted by the closed door, the sound got Timmy's immediate attention.

Daisy motioned with her free hand. "I got to tend to my baby. Come on in if you want." She turned and quickly entered the cabin, leaving the door open.

* * *

Tim walked his horse forward and tethered him to a post. Stepping onto the porch, his boots clunked. He brushed his chaps and duster, removed his hat, and stepped inside his childhood home.

Waves of nostalgia assailed him and in his mind he saw his father and mother sitting in rockers in front of the hearth. He saw himself sitting at their feet and listening to his pa expound on the wonderful lands to the west in Oregon. His father had never made it there, but his descriptions had been amazingly accurate.

Tim glanced from the hearth to Daisy entering the room from the bedroom. She cradled a tiny bundle and her expression of love as she looked at her baby put a lump in his throat.

She glanced up. "This is June. I named her June because it's my favorite month of the year. The weather's warming and flowers and baby animals are springing up everywhere." She stepped close enough for Tim to see the baby's face.

"She's beautiful, Daisy. How old is she?"

"Two months."

Tim wanted to ask where the baby's father was, but didn't know if the question would come across as offensive.

Daisy glanced up and her eyes conveyed the fact that she understood his hesitance. With a sad expression, she said, "I'm not married. So if you want to leave and have nothing to do with me like the rest of the folks around here, the door's open." She finished the sentence with a hint of hostility.

Tim's stare never wavered. "I'm not like most folks."

Daisy studied him for a second. "Please have a seat, Timmy. I need to feed June and then I'll come back and make us some tea." The baby squalled and Daisy lifted her over her shoulder. "There, there, baby girl. Mama's gonna take care of you." She returned to the bedroom and closed the door.

Tim didn't wait for Daisy to return to make tea. He set about finding the ingredients and pouring hot water already on the stove. When she returned, he had the table set with a teapot and cups. His efficiency had disclosed that she had little in the way of food in her cupboards.

Daisy's eyes widened, and then narrowed. "I don't expect guests to do my job."

"No, ma'am. But anyone can see you need a little help around here."

"I don't want any charity."

It was obvious to Tim that he had rankled Daisy's pride. "I don't think me making tea is considered charity." Before she could respond he pulled a chair out for her and said, "I 'spose June's happy as a bug-in-a-rug now. I don't hear anything."

Talking about the baby seemed to distract Daisy and she reached for the teapot, pouring tea for Tim and then herself. "She usually sleeps all afternoon. About three she wakes up and wants to play 'til evening." Daisy lifted her cup and smiled, once again looking lovely.

Tim sipped his own tea and after a few minutes of general conversation decided a direct approach was needed for him to find out the information he wanted. "Who planted your corn?"

"I did some of it, but then I hired a couple of drifters looking for work."

"You mean you planted crops just after having a baby?"

"Not that it's any of your business, but yes; I did what had to be done."

"What about the townsfolk?"

Daisy snorted. "As far as I'm concerned, those folks can have the hell fire they keep tryin' to send me too jus' 'cause I got a babe and no husband. I want nothin' to do with the lot of 'em."

Tim glanced over Daisy's shoulder, made a decision, looked back at her and held her gaze. "What about June's father? Is he alive?"

Firelights sparked in her hazel eyes. "Timmy, I don't see as how that's any of your business, but because I know you from way back, I'll answer what you so obviously want to know. Yes, he's alive. He knows about the babe. But he'll never marry me. Besides, it would be a cold day in hell before I'd marry that rat, even if he begged. Let's just say he was a sweet talker, wantin' one thing from me, and after he got it, I was history in his book."

The fire in her eyes burned brighter and Tim almost looked away. Instead, he said, "Please call me Tim, not Timmy, and thanks for confiding in me. That helps me with my decision."

"What decision?"

"I'm going to stay on and help you get this farm back in shape."

Daisy's eye's widened and she swatted aside a wayward strand of hair that had gotten caught in her mouth. "You'll do no such thing. I already told you I don't accept charity and I'm–"

Tim interrupted. "I heard what you said, but I'm doin' this more for the babe than for the stubborn likes of you."

Daisy jerked back in her chair looking dumbfounded, just what he had intended to happen, and he went for the kill. "You keep working the way you have been and you could end up sick or dead, and then what's to become of your babe. You want her raised by one of those townsfolk you despise? Of course, I know a wonderful orphanage in Oregon that would take her in and love her."

Daisy's mouth gaped and Tim hastily stood. "I'll bunk out in the barn." Before she could respond, he was out the door.

Chapter 4: Fixin' What's Broken

Tim figured that all the talk he'd heard about red-headed gals being stubborn was true. He was a good judge of character and he'd had Daisy pegged from the get-go. She was a proud woman whose pride would either get her sick or dead. He could only imagine the gossip she'd been subjected to that had made her so bitter.

Vividly, he remembered Pastor Pittance's wife, Prudence, from the Oregon Trail. Until the unexpected death of her husband, she'd been a force to be reckoned with. If one didn't fall into her guidebook for morality, she'd make your life miserable. That's what she'd done to his ma.

However, life has a way of turning the tables, and when Mrs. Pittance's husband died after three months on the trail, she'd confessed to an immoral act in her own life. She'd figured part of her penance was to lead everyone onto the path of righteousness. Her efforts, of course, were not welcomed by those she chose to direct them toward. Later, after a complete change of heart, she'd confided that it came about not only because of the death of her husband, but also because of Tim's mother's kindness to everyone, regardless of their sins.

Tim's musings ceased as he unsaddled Amigo and glanced around the barn. There was an old nag in one stall and a milk cow in another; a few chickens squawked and scurried. That was the extent of Daisy's animals.

She doesn't even have a dog for protection.

He shook his head and mentally ticked off needed chores.

By evening, he'd fed the cow and horse from stores of hay and grain that were perilously low. He'd shooed the chickens back into their pen and repaired the wire permitting their escape, and he'd just finished feeding and brushing his own horse when a noise caused him to glance toward the barn entrance. Backlit by soft evening light, Daisy's hair glowed like coals of fire and her dress shifted in the breeze, clinging to her body. She was curvy in all the right places and Tim supposed her large breasts were due to nursing her babe. He coughed when he realized the direction of his thoughts.

Daisy placed her hands on her hips. "I got beans and cornbread ready for supper and a little preserves to sweeten the cornbread. You best come in and eat since it don't look like you're leavin'." She abruptly turned and stalked back to the house.

Tim watched the sway of her hips and shook his head again to dislodge his thoughts. The last thing he needed was entanglement with a woman. Besides, Janie Iverson, whom he'd gone to school with since the age of twelve, was the sweet gal everyone expected him to marry. They'd always had a hankerin' for each other and he'd been thinking about settling down after this trip. He surely didn't need to be gawking at another woman.

He washed up at the well and then returned to the cabin. The door was slightly ajar and when he paused to knock, Daisy said, "No need to knock. Come in and have a seat."

The scent of hot cornbread filled the cabin. "Smells wonderful."

Daisy motioned to a chair at the table and ladled beans into a bowl, topping it with cornbread. She pointed to a jar. "That's wild blackberry preserves. I made it myself last year. It was my ma's recipe and it's tasty as can be."

She dished her own bowl and sat across from him. There was an awkward silence. Tim wasn't sure if she was going to say a blessing and so he waited. She met his gaze and seemed to read his thoughts. "The Good Lord knows I'm thankful for what I have so I don't have to keep telling him. Go ahead and eat."

Tim nodded and lifted a bite of beans to his mouth, followed by a bite of cornbread. "Daisy, this is delicious. I remember your ma was a great cook. Looks like you learned well."

Pink color suffused her face and she glanced at the table. "Thank you."

Daisy's blush intrigued Tim and he secretly watched her. She had a strong nose, expressive hazel eyes, and a pretty mouth. Her hair was dark red and her complexion tanned by the sun, without freckles.

She caught him looking at her. "Is something wrong? Is my face smudged?"

Now Tim turned red knowing he'd been caught staring. "No, ma'am. I was just thinking that your coloring is unusual for a redhead."

She shrugged. "My ma's hair was orange and she had tons of freckles. I don't know what happened to me. I guess–" The baby fussed and she smiled. "I was wondering when my little sweetie was going to wake up. Excuse me while I go feed her."

Tim nodded and watched her rush from the room. Sudden anger started his blood pumping. What man would father a child and then leave the mother and his babe defenseless?

Chapter 5: Meet the Father

Daisy cuddled June as she nursed and thought about Tim. She remembered him as being fun, but also studious and kind; nothing had changed. He had a demeanor that radiated calmness and his quick wit was obvious. As much as she hated accepting charity, she knew she desperately needed help. It was time to bridle her pride. Tim was right. If she wouldn't do it for herself, she had to do it for her child.

Shifting June to her other breast, she closed her eyes and willed her heart rate to slow down. June must have felt the rapid beat because she became restless. Breathing deeply didn't help, so Daisy just gave in to the one remembrance she had been pushing aside—the dream.

"It's ridiculous," she whispered to June. "It was just a coincidence that my mother, grandmother, great-grandmother, and so on as they claimed, all dreamed of the men they would one day marry. Ma always said it was a gift, but it seems more like an old wives' tale to me."

Lifting June over her shoulder to burp, Daisy remembered the day her pa had driven Tim and his mother to meet the stagecoach bound for St. Louis. The night before, she had dreamed of her and Timmy being grown up and standing in front of a preacher repeating wedding vows. Although she hadn't seen their faces clearly, she'd known it was them. After the preacher pronounced them husband and wife, Timmy had placed his hands on either side of her face and bent to kiss her. She'd wakened before his lips touched hers.

The next day on the buckboard she'd foolishly told him about the dream. Of course, being a boy of eight, he'd told her in no uncertain terms that there was no way he was marrying her. He'd been rude and his mother had chastised him for his behavior.

Throughout the years, she had often thought of Timmy and his mother. Daisy's own mother had received a few letters from Mrs. Wells—later Mrs. Jerome—describing their wonderful life in Oregon. After hearing her mother read the letters aloud to her father, Daisy figured she'd never see Timmy again, and even if there was any truth to the "gift" in her maternal lineage, that chain had been broken with her.

When she got pregnant, she thought Jensen would become her husband. How wrong she had been.

June gave a loud burp and Daisy reached for a diaper to change her. Thinking about Jensen put a dark cloud in the room. She had been stupid to believe his lies. In her defense, however, she remembered longing for companionship. Miserable loneliness had brought her defenses down until she was easily manipulated by him.

Daisy placed the safety pin in June's diaper and glanced across the room to the old vanity with its wavy mirror. As always, her unruly hair had escaped its topknot and corkscrew strands hugged her face and neck. She supposed it was the fashion, but it just made her feel unkempt.

Puffing a breath, her thoughts returned to Jensen Logan. Smoothing her hand down June's soft cheek, she whispered, "We don't need him or any man. The only thing I can thank him for is giving me you."

Lifting her baby, Daisy returned to the main room where Tim had already cleared his plate and was rinsing it in the sink. He said without turning around, "Can I warm your coffee?"

His tall presence suddenly made the room seem small and Daisy felt overwhelmed. No man except her father had ever been that kind and helpful. She sat at the table, placed June over her shoulder, and stared at her plate. She knew it was terrible to ask such a thing, but she said, "What do you want from me?"

Rather than become angry, Tim reached for a potholder, gripped the coffee pot, and brought it to the table to refill Daisy's cup and then his. He set the pot back on the stove and answered when he sat down. "I don't want anything from you. Like I said, I'll only stay long enough to help get your farm in shape." He sipped his coffee and appeared thoughtful. "Contrary to what you seem to believe, there are folks who actually want to help others. That's how my ma raised me."

A lump formed in Daisy's throat and she blinked back tears. Quickly turning her attention to June who was kicking and squirming, she said, "I need to put her to bed."

For the remainder of the evening, Tim discussed things around the farm that he intended to take care of, and every time Daisy objected that something was too extravagant, he brushed her objection aside.

That night, as she lay in bed with June cuddled to her body, she did something she hadn't done since Jensen rejected her—she cried.

* * *

A week after barging into Daisy's life, Tim had repaired barn siding, replaced fencing, cleaned animal stalls, hammered new shingles on the roof, and started other chores. Now he chopped wood at the side of the barn. Daisy had come out earlier and brought him water and he couldn't help but notice how she averted her gaze from his naked chest. When he'd removed his shirt, he hadn't been thinking that it might make her uncomfortable. He'd just been so hot. Sluicing water over his face and upper body, he was about to put his shirt back on when he heard a horse approaching. A single rider rode into the yard. From the cocky way he held his body, Tim instantly disliked him. He stepped so the cowboy could see him.

The well-dressed man reined his horse beside Tim. He lifted his hat to smooth a hand through black hair before planting it back on his head. Without introducing himself, he said, "Where's Daisy?"

Tim disliked the man even more. "As soon as you let me know who you are, I'll let her know she has a visitor."

By the cowboy's frown, he had a dislike for Tim also. He snorted, "Visitor? Hell, I'm a lot more than a visitor to that gal." He dismounted, gazed at Tim's naked chest, and said slyly, "And how 'bout yourself? Are you a visitor or warming her bed like I did?"

Tim had learned years ago from his stepfather to always appear calm, even when his insides were churning like butter, and responded evenly, "Either state your business or leave. Neither Daisy, nor I, have time for word games."

Other than a spark in the cowboy's eyes, he also kept a poker face. "You must not be from around here or you'd know who you're talking to."

"Really? Maybe I'm glad to be an out-of-towner 'cause I really don't want to make your acquaintance."

The man's bland expression cracked and he said menacingly, "My name is Jensen Logan and I happen to own most of the countryside around here."

The men were so wrapped up in their animosity that they hadn't heard Daisy step onto the porch. With a laugh that sounded more like a snort, she said, "The hell you do. Your pa owns everything." She paused. "Even you."

Jensen stared at her with hatred. "That mouth of yours is what's kept you an old maid. I'd have married you before the babe was born if not for that."

"That's a crock and you know it. You ran as fast and as far as your lily-livered self could go when you found out. I bet you still haven't told your pa."

A flush crept up Jensen's neck. He glanced at Tim and then back at Daisy. "Who's he? I don't think he needs to hear our dirty laundry."

"He's a friend of mine and welcome here as long as he wants to stay. But you're not. Leave my property before I pull out my shotgun."

Jensen squinted at Daisy. "I want to see the kid."

"Over my dead body."

Jensen ground his teeth. "I got the right."

"You got no rights. You're not my husband and you never will be. Now, I repeat, get off my property."

Jensen threatened, "You haven't heard the last of this, Daisy. I'll not only have your property; I'll have you."

Daisy's red hair seemed to glow brighter when she replied softly, "I'd choose to spend eternity in hell before marrying the likes of you."

Jensen replied, "Who said anything about marriage? You'll not be my wife; you'll be my whore."

Tim's calm demeanor exploded and he rushed the arrogant man, toppling him into the dirt. He struck a blow to the man's face. "Someone needs to teach you manners."

Jensen recovered and sent an uppercut into Tim's jaw, which busted his lip.

The men rolled in the dirt until a shotgun blast broke through the sound of their grunting. Daisy now pointed her weapon at the men. "Both of you stop! Jensen, get off my property!" She lifted the gun toward the sky and fired again.

Both men jumped to their feet and Jensen reached to retrieve his hat, sending Tim a look of hatred. He turned his gaze back on Daisy and said sarcastically, "Later, sweetheart."

Both Daisy and Tim watched Jensen ride away. After he was gone, Daisy turned her wrath on Tim. "That was pure foolishness. That man's pa owns most of the land around here. He can make life miserable."

Tim shot back, "Oh, so you don't think the way you've been living is miserable."

Daisy's mouth gaped, but she didn't retort. She simply turned and strode inside the house. June was now screaming.

Chapter 6: Unexpected News

Over the next week, Tim continued making much needed repairs to the barn and house, worked in the corn field, and mulled over Daisy's situation. He often found himself watching her when she wasn't looking—weeding her garden, washing clothes, beating rugs, collecting eggs, and other necessary chores. How she had managed to keep her farm going for as long as she had without help was beyond Tim's understanding.

By the end of the second week, the place was looking pretty fine and the crop healthy. They ate a lot of beans and cornbread, and although Tim was sick of the same food every day, he never complained. He'd already decided to make a trip to town to stock up on supplies. He knew Daisy would pitch a fit when he returned with a wagonload of necessities bought with his own money, but that was just too bad. Other than reinforcing the fact in his mind that he was simply helping a young mother and her babe, he didn't ponder his motivation.

As for moving on, he'd decided to stay another week to make sure things were running smooth. After that, he planned to leave enough money for Daisy to hire help at harvest time, and then continue southward.

When he'd said goodbye to his family in Oregon, it had been with the intent of visiting his childhood home before riding to Texas to visit his Aunt Lilah and Uncle Rush at their ranch on the Nueces River.

The first time he'd met his Aunt, other than when he was a babe and didn't remember, was five years previous when Rush Garrett, his stepfather's friend, had located her in New Orleans and escorted her to Oregon. Tim's ma and pa had hired Rush to find her because his ma hadn't seen her sister since they were young women. After the death of their parents, the sisters had been forced to sell their farm or lose it. The proceeds had been split and the women pursued different life-journeys. Tim had often heard his mother speak of how much she missed her sister, and when his stepfather suggested they hire Rush to find her, she'd readily agreed.

After Rush had located his Aunt Lilah and convinced her to return to Oregon with him, their train had been held up and Lilah kidnapped. Almost dead by the time Rush rescued her, he had nursed her back to health before continuing onward to Oregon and encountering more adventure than one could expect in a lifetime. Eventually, however, the sisters had been reunited.

Tim smiled when he thought about the happy outcome of his aunt and uncle's misadventures—not only had the sisters been reunited, but Rush and Lilah had fallen in love and returned to Rush's ancestral home in south Texas.

Over the next four years, railroad expansion had exploded and they again traveled to Oregon with their adopted son, Chad, and three year old daughter, Ivy, for a month long visit. That had been only a year previous.

Tim halted Amigo on a rise which gave him an excellent view of the farm his father and mother had built and his heart swelled with pride. He had loved his pa deeply and dreamed of one day returning to this home, if only to put to rest that part of him that had never left. Maybe he could do so now.

During his aunt and uncle's visit, his uncle must have perceived his restless spirit, because he'd offered Tim a job working his ranch. He'd said there was nothing better than hard work and open range for airing out a man's head.

Over the winter months Tim had been thinking a lot about his future, and when spring arrived, he decided to take his Uncle Rush up on his offer. That is, after paying a visit to Missouri. And now he was entwined with Daisy Smithson's problems.

In the distance, Tim saw two riders galloping toward Daisy's farm. He urged Amigo forward.

* * *

Daisy sat in a rocker on the front porch playing with June on her lap. Her baby smiled and the sight always stole her breath. She spoke to her child. "Looks like Tim has this farm in shipshape condition. I think everything is going to turn out just fine. We'll make a profit on our harvest, pay the final farm payment to the bank, and then be free and clear of owing anyone anything. And best of all, we'll have each other."

Daisy knew she was being overly optimistic, but since it was such a beautiful day, she allowed herself that one comfort. Approaching horsemen caught her attention and her optimism disappeared like a magician's rabbit when she recognized one of the riders. Mr. Elijah Logan sat tall and haughty in his saddle. He was probably close to sixty, and other than some extra pounds, most folks would consider him handsome. Jensen was a younger version of his father. Daisy now knew their looks and genial attitudes to be deceiving. They were conniving, selfish men, and she wanted nothing to do with them. She figured the rider behind Mr. Logan was one of the hired hands that always accompanied him. Since the man had never ridden onto her property before, she could only surmise he had found out about his granddaughter.

Daisy's heart pounded and she quickly took June inside to hide under the bed and retrieve her shotgun. Stepping back onto the porch, she glanced around for Tim. She'd seen him ride out earlier. He hadn't said where he was going so he probably wasn't far away. He seemed to like riding her land and she figured he was revisiting old memories.

The two riders paused about twenty feet out from her porch. She raised her gun and Mr. Logan lifted gloved hands into the air. He wore a pained expression, something Daisy had never seen on his face. He said, "May I walk up to the porch?"

Daisy lowered her gun slightly. "Just say what you got to say from where you are."

Another rider galloped into the yard and Daisy sighed with relief when she saw it was Tim. He trotted his horse to the porch, dismounted, and faced Mr. Logan alongside her.

Daisy said, "You can talk in front of him. He's a family friend."

Mr. Logan stated without emotion. "Jensen is dead."

Daisy lowered her gun a little more. "Say again?"

"My son is dead. He was shot in a poker game."

A poker game he was cheating at, Daisy thought, and then felt bad for jumping to such a conclusion about a dead man.

"I'm sorry to hear that, Mr. Logan. I know he was your only child."

Something flickered across the man's face and then he said, "Before Jensen died, he confessed to fathering your child." The man's hard stare bore into Daisy. "That means I have a granddaughter."

Blood rushed to Daisy's ears and her heart pounded. "Just where is this conversation headed, sir?"

"I think you know. I want to meet my granddaughter. If I'd known my boy was the father, he would have married you the day I found out." He made a waving motion toward the cabin. "I can offer my granddaughter a better life than this pitiful farm. I want you and the babe to come live on my ranch. You'll never want for anything."

Daisy lowered the barrel of her rifle until it touched the ground and took a step forward, fire dancing in her eyes. "This *pitiful farm* as you call it, just happens to be my home. The home I love and have no intention of leaving. Now you, Mr. Logan, can leave my *home.* I want nothin' to do with you or yours. I'm sorry about Jensen, but he was a mean man and I imagine instrumental in his own death." Lifting her head proudly, she said, "Good day, sir."

Mr. Logan was not to be deterred. "I got somethin' I want to show you." Slowly, he reached toward his vest pocket and Tim stepped between Daisy and the rancher. Daisy's patience had reached the breaking point and although she appreciated Tim's protective gesture, she said, "Move out of the way, Tim. I got my rifle."

Tim's words floated back to her. "And I've got my colt 45. Just stay where you are, Daisy."

Mr. Logan lifted a paper from his pocket. With eyes like flint, he said, "I thought you might be difficult so I did a little digging in county records. Seems your ma and pa took out a loan on this land a few years back and a payment comes due every year. You're late and the bank is looking the other way until after harvest. That seems to be a might unfair to the rest of us hard-working folk who have to pay our debts on time, so I took it upon myself to have a little talk with Mr. Fletcher at the bank. He realized the error of his ways and sent me here as his representative to collect payment. You have until noon, three days hence, to pay or lose your land. Of course, if you and the babe were to come to my ranch, I could pay your debt and keep the land in the family."

The audacity of the man stunned Daisy and for a second she didn't react, but when she did, she stepped around Tim, lifted her gun, and shouted, "You lily-livered, piss-poor excuse for a man. If you don't get off my property this minute I'll shoot your ass into the next county. I'll–"

Tim jerked the rifle from Daisy's hands. The cowboy accompanying Mr. Logan now had his revolver unholstered and pointed at them.

Tim said, "Tell him to holster his gun. They'll be no showdown here. There's a babe inside." He ordered without looking at Daisy. "Go inside, Daisy!"

Daisy sputtered. "If he thinks that I'm going to–"

Tim repeated forcefully, "Go inside the house, Daisy!"

The howl of the baby startled everyone and Daisy felt some of her fire leave her. Without another word, she turned and entered the house.

* * *

Tim watched Mr. Logan make a motion and his companion holstered his gun. Still holding Daisy's rifle, he said tightly, "Leave this property and don't ever return."

The older man touched the brim of his hat. "In three days the property's mine. I'll have access to my own flesh and blood, come hell or high water, and that little spitfire won't stop me. Have I made myself clear?"

Tim repeated, "I suggest you leave because you're trespassing. I'd love to shoot you into the next county just like Daisy said."

Mr. Logan motioned to his companion and they swiftly turned and galloped away. Tim hung his head. That gal's temper was sure to get her in deep trouble. He turned to enter the cabin, but Daisy rushed out the door with the baby held over her shoulder. June was squalling up a storm.

Daisy was none to happy herself. She spat, "I'll not have you fighting my battles, Timmy Wells."

Tim shook his head. "It's Tim, not Timmy. We're not eight years old anymore."

Daisy was not to be denied her say. The baby screamed louder and she said over the top of her cries, "Regardless, you're interfering where you've not been invited."

Suddenly, Tim smiled, which stopped Daisy's tirade. "Daisy Smithson, you are one Missouri Challenge, that's for sure. Go in the house and comfort June while I think this through."

Grabbing Amigo's reins he led him to the barn while listening to Daisy's sputters, which made him smile even more.

Chapter 7: Plan A

Tim spent the rest of the afternoon considering ways around Daisy's dilemma. By the time dusk blanketed the land, he had a plan. Daisy was going to hit the roof when she heard it, but she didn't have much choice. He left the barn and knocked on the cabin door.

Daisy yanked the door open. "It's about time you showed up. I was just about to come get you. Supper's getting cold."

Tim attempted a joke. "But your temper's not, right?"

"Not what?"

"Getting cold."

Daisy smoothed her hands down her skirt, closed her eyes, opened them again, and said, "I don't know what's gotten into you, but maybe it's time you were on your way. You've done more than enough and I'm truly grateful, but I–"

"–can take care of yourself, right?" Tim interrupted.

Daisy stood a little taller. "Yes. That's right."

Tim walked past her and sat at the table. He stirred the beans in his bowl. He was sick of beans and wondered if Daisy could cook anything else.

Gingerly, she sat across from him.

Tim finished his meal in a few bites, pushed away from the table, and walked to the stove. Lifting the coffee pot with a cloth, he warmed his cup and then

Daisy's before sitting back down. Leaning forward, he said, "I believe I have a solution to your dilemma."

Daisy narrowed her eyes.

"But I'm warning you, you're not going to like it."

By now she was practically squinting.

Inhaling a breath, he blurted, "We get married and I pay your debt to the bank."

Daisy shot out of her chair. "What!"

In a calm voice, he said, "Sit down Daisy while I explain."

"I'm not marrying anyone. I've had my fill of lies from men. I'll roast in hell before–"

"Sit down, Daisy, and hear me out." His calm voice turned commanding and broke through her tirade. Warily, she perched at the edge of her chair.

Tim continued, "We both love this land. My pa and ma built the farm and yours expanded it. It would be a shame to lose it to the likes of Mr. Logan, which will probably happen unless something is done. After meeting the man, I'm sure his reach into the community and even the county is as powerful as you warned. Of course, I'll talk to the bank president to verify what he's saying is true about the note on your land, but I have a feeling he's not lying. Am I right?"

Daisy stared mutely at him.

"Anyway, hear me out," he repeated. "Marriage is not necessarily forever, and the reason I know this is because my stepfather got a divorce from his first wife. It's not often done, but it is possible."

Daisy's eyes widened and she opened her mouth to speak.

Tim lifted his hand to keep her quiet. "By marrying me, two problems are solved. Mr. Logan cannot lay claim to the land or June. She'll have a legal father and the land will be yours free and clear because I'll not put my name on the title. After a few months, when this mess blows over, we'll talk about a divorce," he paused, "if we still want one." He leaned back in his chair, stretched his legs out, and waited for Daisy's response.

* * *

Daisy rarely felt at a loss for words, but this was one of those times. She simply stared at Tim with her jaw slack. Finally, she whispered, "That's got to be the craziest idea I've ever heard."

His tiny smile sent her heart racing and she remembered her dream of marrying him.

He said softly, "I didn't say it wasn't crazy."

Daisy recovered her composure. "No. No. Absolutely not."

Tim shrugged. "Have it your way and lose your land, because I come with the money to pay off the debt. I'll not pay the bank and then leave you and June to the likes of Mr. Logan. And you know as well as I, he'll not leave off his claim against the child after losing his only son. He's the kind of man who has to prove himself the victor in everything. Whoever he squashes along the way makes little difference to him."

Tim stood, drained his coffee cup, and said as he turned to leave. "If you won't think of your own wellbeing, at least think of June's."

Before Daisy could retort, he was gone.

All night, Daisy tossed and turned, dreaming of her baby being ripped from her arms. By morning she was more exhausted than when she had gone to bed. Sitting on the edge of her bed, she comforted her cranky baby. She smoothed a hand down June's silky cheek. She would do anything to protect her child. The lump in Daisy's throat seemed to be there perpetually.

With a sigh of resolve, she knew she had no other option than the one Tim proposed. She had no money to pay the bank. She was living on borrowed time. Last year Mr. Fletcher had let her slide a few months until after harvest, but with Elijah Logan riding his tail, it was hopeless. The bank *would* repossess her land if she didn't pay within three days.

With a heavy heart, Daisy wondered if her life was meant to be one ordeal after another. What had happened to that carefree and happy childhood that had once been hers?

Chapter 8: Surprise

Two days later, Daisy watched Tim reach into his pocket for the ring he'd purchased at the general store in the next county. He smiled reassuringly and placed it on her finger. The witness standing beside Daisy in the judge's chamber in that same county, a rotund middle-aged woman named Myrtle Beckenworth, held June while the ceremony took place. The judge said a few more words that she didn't pay attention to because her head was dizzy from the enormity of what she was doing.

With a voice ripe with censor because there was already a child, the judge proclaimed, "I now pronounce you husband and wife. Mr. Wells, you may kiss Mrs. Wells."

When Daisy couldn't bring herself to look at Tim, he gently placed his hands on either side of her face and tilted her head upward. Her eyes widened as his face descended—just like in her dream. He lightly kissed her lips and moved his mouth to her ear. Softly, he said, "It'll be okay, Daisy."

The witness holding June cooed at the baby and June laughed. Immediately, Daisy's attention was riveted on her child. She said with excitement, "Did you hear that? That's her first outright laugh?"

The kindly witness said, "She's happy her pa and ma have tied the knot. Here you go, sir. Here's your baby girl." She handed the baby to Tim and he grinned when June smiled up at him and laughed again.

Daisy blinked back tears and did not correct the woman's assumption that June was Tim's child. He held her baby as if it were an often occurrence, cradling her in one arm. He glanced at Daisy. "My ma had two children after me and made me help in their care." He winked. "She even made me change diapers."

Tim's joking lightened the weight Daisy was feeling. She replied, "So I can count on you to change even the worst of diapers when we get home."

Tim's gaze held hers. "You sure can, darlin'."

Daisy's heart thumped at the intensity of his stare and she quickly looked away. Mrs. Beckenworth grinned broadly and even the judge's expression softened. He said, "Congratulations! Now we just need to sign a couple of documents and you newlyweds can be on your way."

Tim kissed June's forehead and handed her to Daisy. He said, "After we sign the papers we should celebrate before leaving town."

Mrs. Beckenworth interjected, "I know the best diner, too."

When Daisy walked beside Tim toward *Verna's Supper House,* she wanted to pinch herself to see if she was dreaming. After they were seated, Tim told her to order whatever she wanted. As for himself, he said he was having steak and baked potato with a mound of hot biscuits dripping butter. Daisy's mouth watered. She hadn't tasted a juicy steak in months. Suddenly feeling shy, she said, "I'll have the same."

Tim shifted his gaze back to the menu. "And what would you like for dessert, Mrs. Wells?"

Daisy inhaled sharply at her new title and pretended to study her menu.

Tim leaned forward. "Choose anything your heart desires."

Daisy forced herself to read the delicious selections: apple pie, buttermilk pie, boysenberry pie, pecan pie, and cinnamon buns. She lifted her eyes to his. "I absolutely adore pecan pie."

"Then that's what you'll have."

"What about you? What are you having?"

"I think I'll have a slice of apple pie *and* boysenberry. Would you like to add another dessert?"

"Goodness, no. I don't know if I can eat all this food as it is." She laughed. "I see you didn't order beans."

Tim grinned and made a face. "You can order beans if you're overly fond of them."

"And here I thought you had a hankerin' for them."

"Don't get me wrong. You make a mean pot of legumes; but everyday?"

Daisy shifted June in her arms and stared lovingly at her sleeping face. Without lifting her head, she said, "I just want to thank you for going to all this trouble. I know you've put your life on hold. Most men would have galloped away faster'n a cockroach being chased, and I—well, just don't have words to express my thanks." She felt a flush creep up her neck. Quickly glancing at Tim and then back at June, her stomach did flip-flops at the emerald sparkle in his eyes.

"Daisy, I couldn't live with myself if I didn't help you." He chuckled. "Looks like your dream came true."

Daisy's face flamed. "Please don't put any weight to that dream. It was a little girl's fantasy." Before Tim could respond, a plump, rosy-faced, older woman came to take their orders.

* * *

The day after his marriage, Tim left the bank with the deed to Daisy's land in hand. It had taken most of his money, but now she owned her land free and clear. He couldn't wait to tell her.

With a happy heart, he drove her old buckboard that he'd also repaired, to the front of *Jebson's General Store*. He intended to load up on staples, buy a ribbon for Daisy's hair, a doll for June, and then hope for a bountiful harvest to replenish his funds. Daisy's corn field looked excellent and there was no reason to believe it wouldn't be a bumper crop. Next year, he would enlarge the field and use the planting practices his mother had taught him.

Thinking about his mother made Tim smile. She was a farmer through-and-through. Her bountiful harvests were legendary and she was often visited by growers begging to know her secrets. During their first year in Oregon City, he remembered how the townsfolk had scoffed at a woman farming alone. Soon they'd eaten their words.

After that first harvest, Cooper Jerome had returned and married his mother, and together they were a force to be reckoned with. In their sixteen years of marriage, except for a couple of years of drought, they had produced the best crops in their county, possibly in their state.

Tim jumped from the buckboard saying a silent thank you to his ma and stepfather for teaching him everything they'd learned over the years. With a skip in his step, he entered the mercantile. He'd visited a few times since his return and reacquainted himself with his childhood friends, Zack and Zeke Jebson, who now jointly owned the store. Things hadn't changed much in seventeen years—the Jebson family, which included cousins and uncles, still owned just about all the businesses in town.

"Howdy, Timmy," said Zeke.

Tim grinned and didn't correct his name. Cooper had been the first person to call him Tim and not Timmy. When his mother had asked Cooper why, he'd explained that Timmy was a boy's name—Tim was a man's name—and because of his pa's death her boy was having to grow up fast. At the age of eight, Timmy became Tim.

"Howdy, Zeke. How have you been? How's your wife and children?"

"We're well and happy. In fact, my Cindy just told me we're expectin' another child. That'll make four. We only need one more babe to catch up with Zack's five."

Tim chuckled. "I must say, your family is one of the most prolific I've ever encountered. No wonder you own most of the town."

Zeke laughed. "I think owning businesses is in our blood. Just like farming is in yours. I remember my pa talkin' about how beautiful your farm was when you lived here. The Smithsons kept it looking good, too, but never had quite the crop your ma and pa did. After their deaths, I know Daisy did her best." He lowered his voice. "But with that unfortunate business…" His voice trailed. "Anyway, most folks in town turned their backs on her when she refused to marry any of the callers willin' to accept her bastard child. Folks were up in arms thinkin' a woman shouldn't turn away her only chance of makin' herself respectable. I prob'ly woulda' sided with the townsfolk 'ceptin I knew the men offering for her hand. Mostly, they just wanted to add more help to runnin' their own farms. There wasn't an honorable man in the bunch. And besides that, what young gal wants to marry an old fart at least twice her age."

Tim listened with interest.

Zeke finished with. "I think it's right honorable of you fixin' her place and helpin' get her crop in this year. Even though some of my family put pressure on me to cut her credit when she refused to marry, I never did. She might be a bit late in payin' her bill, but she's always paid. I considered it my Christian duty to treat her right."

Tim had decided it would be best to keep his marriage a secret for the time being. If not, he would have gladly announced it to Zeke. But he knew how fast gossip travels and he didn't want to borrow trouble. Mr. Logan would be livid when he found out. Instead, he said, "I know Daisy appreciates everything you've done. Now how about we start loading supplies?"

* * *

Just as he had threatened, Mr. Logan and his hired hand showed up to collect on the debt to the bank. Tim ordered Daisy to stay in the cabin. Of course, she didn't listen, and followed him onto the porch carrying her rifle. Tim gave her an exasperated look and then returned his attention to their uninvited guest.

Mr. Logan said, "I guess you know why I'm here. He reached in his pocket and withdrew the collection notice."

Tim lazed against the porch post and studied the man. Mr. Logan shifted his gaze to Daisy. "Well, Daisy, have you reconsidered my offer?"

"Nothin' to reconsider. My answer was no three days ago, and it still is. Now get off my property."

"Sorry, no can do, little lady. Since you've defaulted on your note, I now call it due and I'll be buying your farm from the bank and tearing down these pitiful buildings, your cabin included. Of course, you and the babe got a home with me." His horse whinnied and stepped sideways. "Better think long and hard about what I'm offering. That babe's gonna need a roof over her head." He tipped his hat and started to turn his horse away.

Tim stepped from the post. "Before you celebrate, I think you should know that Daisy now owns this property free and clear. Seems there's no longer a note to collect on."

Mr. Logan jerked his horse back around. The horse snorted and pranced, none to happy with his treatment.

Tim scratched his forehead. "If you don't believe me, you can check with the bank, which you should have done in the first place. I guess you made the long ride out here for nothin'."

Mr. Logan trotted his horse up to Tim, who had stepped off the porch. He glanced first at Tim and then Daisy. With a scowl he said, "You ain't heard the last of this. I got rights to that child. There ain't a judge in the county who'll go against me."

Tim merely shrugged. "Visit any judge you want, but as Daisy's husband, my rights far exceed yours. By law, I'm the child's father and you, sir, don't have a pot to pee in. Now get off my wife's property." Although a command, his voice had not risen in volume.

Mr. Logan's face suffused with rage and his horse sidestepped, obviously feeling the animosity brewing. He stared long and hard at Tim and then Daisy. "I'll have that child," he said, before jerking the reins of his horse and galloping away, followed by his hired hand.

Tim puffed air and turned to see Daisy staring at him with respect. She said, "For being such a studious and quiet man, you sure got a way of puttin' the fear of God into people."

Tim sighed. "Daisy, next time I ask you to stay in the house, will you please listen?" He didn't wait for a response. He just walked to his horse, mounted, and followed their uninvited guests to make sure they were, indeed, leaving the property.

Chapter 9: Plan B

Daisy woke at first light and stretched lazily. June still slept cuddled against her heart and she smoothed her hand down the baby's downy hair that was more red than black. She smiled and listened to morning sounds of birds singing cheerily. Her rooster crowed.

Six weeks of bliss. In another week they would begin harvest and it looked to be bountiful. Even now, knowing her property belonged to her, she still had an inclination to pinch herself to make sure she wasn't dreaming.

As for dreaming, she'd had a recurring one since her wedding, with Tim being the main attraction. In her dream, she was forever on the verge of kissing him when she awakened. It was both frustrating and unnerving. Although she had no control over her dreams, she scolded herself for having them. Tim was simply helping her out of a difficult situation and they would divorce after her situation stabilized.

He didn't say we would divorce for a fact.

Daisy knew she was giving in to girlhood fantasies and should push them aside.

He's so smart and handsome; he wouldn't give me a second glance if circumstances were different.

She reached across June and smoothed a hand down the other side of her bed. What would it feel like to have Tim sleeping beside her, kissing her, touching her?

"Stop it!" She whispered forcefully and woke June.

After feeding her baby, she stepped into the main room where Tim was already stoking a fire in the potbelly stove. He reached for the coffee makings and Daisy said, "Let me make your coffee. In fact, I'll fix you the best breakfast you've ever eaten."

* * *

Tim looked at Daisy carrying June on her hip and his heart melted a little more. She often worked outside without her bonnet and the sun had enhanced the red hues of her pretty hair. Although she had fashioned a topknot, the unruly curls were already escaping.

June looked at him, grinned, and started kicking her legs like she was running. Tim said, "She'll probably walk before she's a year old."

Daisy handed him the baby. "That breakfast comes with childcare duties."

Tim bounced June into the air and she laughed loudly. "I'll gladly trade cooking for baby bouncing."

Daisy inspected their cupboard. "I haven't seen so many staples since pa died. I'll just run to the chicken coop and get eggs."

"Already done." He motioned to the sink.

Within the hour, Daisy had baked biscuits, flipped flapjacks, fried potatoes to crispiness, stirred cornmeal mush, and scrambled eggs. Tim placed June in the cradle he'd built and joined Daisy at the table.

By now, more of her hair had tumbled to her shoulders and he wanted to stroke its silkiness. Happiness had altered her expression and she looked so pretty he had to glance away to keep from pulling her into his arms and kissing her passionately. For several days now, he had been wondering if they could make a go of their marriage. Janie Iverson, his gal back in Oregon City, had never made him feel the way Daisy did. Daisy had a way of stirring his emotions until they ran the gamut from frustrated to edgy to happy to passionate and everything in between.

He said, "You've outdone yourself, darlin'."

She turned pink at his praise and he almost told her how much he wanted to kiss her and become her husband in every way.

June laughed and redirected their attention. Daisy walked to pick her up and returned to the table. She said, "Another week and we'll be harvesting, don't you think?"

"I do. And it's going to be plentiful. I've been thinking that after the harvest, maybe we should take a little time off. Would you like to go to St. Louey for a couple of days? Shop for clothing for you and June?"

Daisy's eyes lit. "I haven't been to the city in years. Maybe we could go to the theater and watch one of those dramas that the newspapers write about or see one of those magic shows."

Tim had a sudden yearning to treat Daisy to whatever she wanted. He looked away before she could see the compassion in his eyes. Here was a young woman who had been struggling for years just to survive, so, of course, she would want to do what all young women dreamed of. He swallowed the lump in his throat and looked back at her with a smile. "You make a list of whatever you want to do, honey, and we'll do it all."

* * *

Daisy felt immobilized by Tim's brilliant green eyes. When she was eight years old, she'd thought him to be the handsomest boy she'd ever met, and as a man, he was the stuff of a young woman's dreams—tall, broad shouldered and lean hipped, with long lashes over kind eyes. His wavy blond hair, reaching his shoulders, contrasted sharply with his tanned face and body. Quite simply, he took her breath away. Often, she secretly watched him when he removed his shirt and washed up at the well, dreaming of touching his beautiful body.

A sudden gust of wind blew the door open, startling both of them and making the baby cry. Tim jumped up to close it while Daisy calmed June. He said, "Looks like storm clouds are moving in fast. Guess we'll get some rain. I better check on the animals and make sure everything's fastened down."

"Okay. I'll start clearing the dishes. We have enough food left over for lunch."

"And dinner," Tim chuckled.

An hour later, he returned and had to hold the door to keep it from blowing off its hinges. Although he smiled, Daisy could see worry reflected in his eyes. He said, "We may need to move to the cellar if the storm gets worse. Why don't you gather anything you and the baby might need?"

"Okay, if you think so."

Within fifteen minutes, the wind was so fierce they could hear shingles being blown off the roof. Daisy's heart raced as she cuddled June and rocked her before the cold hearth.

As he did every few minutes, Tim walked to one of the windows and lifted the plank used in inclement weather. Daisy heard his sharp intake of air and jerked her head toward him.

His face registered alarm, but he said calmly, "Honey, we got a tornado coming this way. We need to head out the back door and into the cellar *now.*" Before he finished talking he was beside her reaching for June.

Daisy's feet took to flight and she rushed to safety behind Tim. Between the cellar and the cabin was a space of about ten feet and the wind almost knocked her off her feet. Tim handed June to her so he could unlatch and lift the cellar door. The wind seemed to have a mind of its own and fought him. Daisy's dress whipped around her and she bent over June to protect her. Finally, he held the cellar door up and she darted inside, careful not to trip on the stairs.

Tim followed her and struggled to shut them inside. By the time he'd secured the latches, Daisy had descended the dozen stairs and stood in the center of a ten by ten underground room. With the door shut, the room was dark except for a couple of cracks emitting weak light. Daisy held her screaming child and waited for Tim to join them.

She heard him fumble with the lantern that was kept in a cubbyhole beside the stairs and whisper a curse before he finally got it lit. The wind howled above them and something thumped on the ground. Daisy jumped and laid her face against June's. "We're okay, sweetheart. Soon, the storm will pass and everything will be normal again."

Tim descended the stairs and hung the lantern from a hook on the ceiling. He pulled a couple of old chairs toward Daisy and said above the howl of the wind, "Honey, why don't you sit and see if you can comfort June. Maybe try feeding her."

"All right." With shaking hands she spread the baby's blanket over her chest, unfastened her dress, and exposed her breasts to her baby. June was so upset she wouldn't nurse. Frustration, as much as the storm, brought tears to Daisy's eyes.

Tim must have been watching because he pulled his chair in front of hers and reached to finger a tear. "Please don't cry, sweetheart."

Another loud thump, and wind so loud it sounded like a banshee, caused Daisy to lean forward and press her body against Tim's. He felt so warm and safe and she was tired of trying to be strong. He enfolded her and June in his powerful embrace and touched his lips to her ear. "I'll take care of you. I promise."

After that, June found a breast to suckle and ceased crying. The blanket slipped to Daisy's waist and Tim's mouth moved from her ear, across her face, and molded to her lips. His hand came up and cupped her free breast.

Daisy no longer heard the storm or felt fearful; she only knew she wanted to stay in her husband's embrace forever. The kiss was long and sweet, and afterward he pulled the blanket back over her and held her while the wind howled. She closed her eyes and rested against him. The storm raged, but she was hardly aware of it until Tim said, "Listen."

There was no sound.

He moved his mouth back to hers. "We're in the eye of the storm." He kissed her again in the silence.

Suddenly, all hell broke loose and the wind screamed and the ground shook. Then it was over.

Tim leaned back and June started fussing. The blanket had slipped again and Daisy glanced down at her exposed bosom. She quickly covered herself.

Tim stood and moved to the stairs. Carefully, he unlatched the door and peeked outside. Light entered through the opening and Daisy saw blue sky. It was as if there had never been a storm. Pushing the cellar door open all the way, he climbed the remainder of the stairs until his upper body was outside. Daisy saw him turn in a circle. By now, she had her bodice buttoned and June cradled and silent. He descended the stairs.

"How bad?" she asked.

His expression revealed the worst. "We'll rebuild, honey."

With a cry, Daisy jumped up and handed the baby to Tim, climbed the stairs, and peeked her head out the opening.

"No!" she whispered in disbelief, and then she cried loudly, "No! No! No!"

There was nothing left of her home but the chimney. As for the barn and outbuildings, siding lay like rubble across the fields.

Almost nothing of their crop remained.

Daisy sank onto the top step and placed her face in her hands. What had started out as one of the happiest days of her life had suddenly turned into another nightmare. She figured she was cursed.

Tim handed June back to her and stepped past her to pace the property. Such was the destruction that she knew rebuilding would take an enormous amount of time and money and there was no way she could ask that of him. Besides, she didn't know if he had any money left after spending so much on the farm. He was a good man and she needed to release him from her cursed life. She'd either have to accept Mr. Logan's offer or sell her land and move on. Maybe she could find work in St. Louis.

Tim returned while she was contemplating her dilemma and crouched beside her.

"Daisy," he whispered.

Her lips trembled as she resolved to tell him he was free to leave; that they had done their best, but he needed to go on with his life. He needed to get the divorce he had spoken of before.

Tim took both her hands in his and said with a little smile. "I have a plan."

Daisy shook her head. "No, Tim. I've decided to sell the land and move to St. Louis. You're free to leave. I can't tie you up with my problems. I'm nothing but trouble."

His smile turned into a frown. "What kind of man do you believe me to be? Do you think I would turn my back on my wife and child?"

Daisy's eyes widened. "Our marriage is a mockery and June isn't your child. I'll not hold you to it."

Slowly, Tim reached and placed his big palm behind Daisy's neck and pulled her cheek to his chest. He bent to whisper in her ear. "Here's the plan, honey. It will work. It's a good one and you'll be able to keep your land."

A sob erupted from Daisy and Tim placed both his arms around her, holding her and June against his solid chest. When her crying was spent and she hiccupped, he said, "When I left Oregon, my plan was to come and visit my childhood home for nostalgic reasons. After that, I was headed to my Aunt Lilah's place in south Texas. She and her husband, Rush Garrett, visited Oregon a year back. He told me I have a job at their ranch, the Big G, anytime I want. He said he would pay me well and the money would help out when I decided to start a family." He stroked Daisy's back. "I've been thinking about settling down, and well, you and June have jumped into my heart something fierce."

Daisy pulled away in shock. "How can you say that? You probably have a girl waiting for you back home. I can't ask—"

Tim placed a finger over Daisy's lips to still her response. He studied her face with a concentration that made her try to look away, but his other hand reached to cup her chin so she couldn't. He said softly, "My mother once told me that her dear friend, Clarissa, someone she met on the Oregon Trail, told her something she's never forgotten. My mother had been battling her love for Cooper because she felt guilty. My pa had only been dead a short time and she didn't think it right to feel something for another man so soon, but Clarissa guessed what she was going through and told her, "The heart can't be tamed." Tim brushed aside a strand of hair that had fallen across Daisy's face. "You have my heart, Daisy. I love you."

Daisy's mouth gaped. "Oh, no. You don't know what you're saying. You're a good man and deserve so much more–"

Again, Tim stopped her protest. Only this time he did it with kisses. Daisy knew she should push him away, but her love for him was too strong. That night, in the cellar, Daisy and Tim turned their mockery of a marriage into a real one.

Two days later, after rounding up the animals that had survived, including Tim's horse, Amigo, and salvaging what they could, they sold Amigo to Zeke Jebson and their other animals and goods to other Jebsons. They used the money to purchase train tickets on the Frisco Railroad out of St. Louis that would bring them to Fort Worth in Texas. From there they would ride the Fort Worth and Denver City Railway to a small town north of Laredo called Harper to be met by Tim's relatives. He sent a wire announcing their arrival and then with jubilant hearts, they began the first leg of their journey as a readymade family.

PART TWO: BIG G RANCH
Chapter 10: Banter

Trent Garrett pulled his buckboard to the front of the general store. In the past five years, the small community of Harper had gone from being a stagecoach stop in the middle of nowhere to a depot for the Fort Worth and Denver City Railway. The town had expanded from a general store, livery, and blacksmith, to now boasting a fancy hotel, theater, dressmaker, diner, postmaster, boarding house, bank, and various other businesses, as well as several brick and clapboard homes.

Trent loaded the bed of the buckboard with supplies and then headed toward the small post office. His brother, Rush, and sister-in-law, Lilah, corresponded frequently with her family in Oregon and they had given him a letter to mail.

Inside the post office, Chuck Wiggins, the postmaster, said, "Howdy Trent. Good to see you. How's your family?"

Trent smiled at the friendly man. "Everyone's healthy and happy. Rush and Lilah's four year old, Ivy, is over the moon about her new pony and Chad's got a grin from here to the east coast after getting a Stetson for his thirteenth birthday."

Mr. Wiggins chuckled. "If Rush and Lilah don't watch out, they'll spoil them kids. Now, I can say that 'cause I got six of my own and want to give them everything, much to the vexation of my wife."

Trent laughed. "I'll share your words of wisdom." He gave Mr. Wiggins' the letter to be posted and the postmaster handed him a small stack of mail before turning and grabbing a slip of paper from a cubbyhole on the back wall. "You also got this wire all the way from Missouri."

Curious, Trent read:

COMING TO WORK RANCH. BRINGING WIFE AND BABE. WILL EXPLAIN THEN. ARRIVE 15 SEPT.
TIM WELLS.

Trent said, "Looks like Lilah's nephew and his family are coming. I didn't know he'd married." He tucked the paper in his pocket. "It'll be nice having another family at the ranch."

Chuck said, "By the way, have you heard from Lilah's friend, Mary Jones? My Sadie said she and Lilah are the best seamstresses in the county. We sure was sorry to see her go. My kids always looked forward to her Sunday School lessons."

"I know what you mean. Everyone at Big G misses her, too. Heck, she worked for Lilah for years in New Orleans and lived with us for four years. We got a letter a while back that said she's settling in just fine as head mistress of the Pittance Orphanage. She said the founder's health is failing and she's trying to learn everything before the woman passes. I guess it was fate that Mary decided to travel to Oregon with Rush and Lilah and the kids last year; otherwise she never would have met Mrs. Pittance."

"Yep, ya never know what fate has in store for ya."

"So true. See you next trip to town, Chuck. Give my best to your family." He returned to his buckboard and headed home. Several miles into his property, he turned off the main road and onto a wide trail that led to the Cayson soddy. At one time, the Caysons had been considered squatters. However, a few years back Trent had taken the advice of his brother and drawn up leases for the four squatter families on their land. Along with leasing the land for a reasonable amount, he'd included a clause deeding the property to them in twenty years if they kept up their end of the agreement and abided by certain guidelines, one of which was to not steal cattle from Big G. Mr. Cayson was prone to drink and Trent had suspected the man of occasional rustling.

Since drawing up the contracts, he hadn't encountered any problems. The families were so thankful knowing one day they would own the land they worked that they had become watchdogs over Big G land. In the years since the contracts were signed, occasional rustlers had attempted to steal cattle, but the former squatters had either waylaid the thieves or warned Trent and Rush. It appeared that both the Ranch and the leaseholders had entered into a mutually beneficial arrangement.

As he pulled to the Caysons' sod house and set the brake, he saw Arizona hoeing the garden. His heart gave its usual kick—something he always ignored—as he jumped from the buckboard. He watched her pause, wipe her hands on her apron, and lean against her hoe.

The day was hot and Trent silently cursed that she was working so hard. She had brothers that should be caring for the garden. When he came close, he noticed her dirt-streaked face beneath the wide brim of her bonnet and rivulets of perspiration running down her neck and chest, disappearing under her bodice. She reached in her pocket for a hankie and swiped at the perspiration.

"Howdy, Trent. What brings you out our way?"

He didn't respond directly to her question. Instead, he frowned. "Where are your brothers; they should be doing the hoeing." Arizona slipped her hankie back in her pocket and grinned. Trent had always thought her smile pretty and his heart kicked again. He ignored it.

Years earlier, he had sworn to never love a woman the way he had loved Katy. Katy had been his brother's wife and Trent's love for her had ended in disaster, with her dying in childbirth alongside his baby. His fornication had resulted in a twenty year separation from his brother. It had only been five years since the brothers reconciled and Rush returned to Big G.

Arizona said, "Tad and Slim went to Laredo with pa. Marty left two months ago to, I suppose, sow his wild oats. But you already know about Marty."

"What are your pa and brothers doing in Laredo when they have a ranch to care for? How long will they be gone?"

Irritation flashed in Arizona's eyes. "Not that it's any of your business, but they went to size up a prize bull for sale. We made a profit the last cattle drive and need another stud—Willy is too old and cranky and doesn't want to perform much anymore."

Trent removed his gaze from Arizona's. He was a rancher and used to the mating habits of animals, and Arizona was a ranch woman, but damn, the woman had his blood heated.

She shifted her stance and asked again, "What brings you out here?"

"Since I was in town, I asked the postmaster if he had mail for you. I thought I'd do a neighborly deed and deliver it."

Arizona grinned and placed her hands on her generous hips. Although she was a short woman, she wasn't tiny like Katy had been. She had curves and a large bosom.

"Well?" she asked. "Do we have mail?"

"Oh, yes. Sorry. My mind took to traveling." He reached inside his vest and removed a catalogue.

Arizona's eyes lit as she reached for it. "I've been waiting for this!"

Rush glanced at the ordinary catalogue and wondered what was so special about it.

Unexpectedly, she blushed and added, "It has that new-fangled appliance that makes washing clothes so much easier."

Trent studied Arizona's face. Why was she blushing over a washer?

She tucked the catalogue into her apron pocket. "Would you like to come inside and have a glass of tea?"

He was about to decline, but changed his mind. After all, it was the hottest part of the day. "Sure, that would be nice." He added, "And it will get you out of the sun."

Arizona frowned. "You should save your gentlemanly instincts for a frail, willowy woman. As you can see, I'm as sturdy as a horse."

Trent shook his head. "Arizona, you are the most forthright woman I have ever met. I can't believe some of the things that come out of your mouth."

She laughed and motioned him toward the soddy. "You've been chastising me for years and you know I never pay attention. Maybe we should call a truce. I'll watch my mouth if you stop harping at me."

"See, there you go. You just made my point."

* * *

Arizona set her hoe against the back of the soddy. Trent outpaced her to the door and held it open. He was a gentleman through-and-through, and since the age of twelve, when she'd first laid eyes on him, he'd stolen her heart. During her teen years, she'd fantasized about becoming his wife and living in his grand house—hell, she'd live in a shack with him—but by the time she was twenty, she'd known he would never give her a second glance. Over the years she'd heard rumors about his infidelity with his brother's beautiful wife and that the babe she'd died birthing had been his, but the story hadn't made her think any less of him. If anything, she had romanticized about a man who loved so deeply that no other woman could take the place of the one he'd lost.

After she'd come to grips with the fact they would never be anything but friends, she'd settled for the banter that flowed between them. To others he seemed quiet and serious, but she knew beneath his imposing exterior was a wonderful sense of humor.

Inside her home, she said, "Have a seat and give me a minute." Even though the soddy she shared with her father and brothers was small, she had draped off rooms to serve as bedrooms; one for her pa, one for her, and another for her brothers. She slipped behind the drape to her room and pulled the catalogue from her pocket, placing it on her lumpy bed. She couldn't wait to look through the readymade dresses. Once a year the Big G Ranch hosted a hoedown for the community and she had been saving since the last one to purchase a new dress.

Reaching for the tiny mirror on her wobbly nightstand, she almost shrieked when she saw her reflection. She had dirt streaked across both cheeks and down her neck and chest. Removing her bonnet and reaching for a cloth, she wet it in her water pitcher and cleaned up. She smoothed her hair and pinched her cheeks. She wondered if the catalogue had some of those fancy face paints that women used to give their cheeks color. Maybe she'd have enough money left over for a small jar.

Inhaling a calming breath, she returned to the table where Trent was already perched on a chair. Reaching inside a lower cabinet where she kept the only items left from her mother, she lovingly retrieved two of the five remaining crystal glasses and poured tea that she'd brewed that morning. She handed one to Trent and sat across from him.

He sipped, and joked, "Arizona, you make the best tea I've ever tasted. But don't tell Pearl I said that."

"I may be able to make tea, but Pearl can sure cook. Her biscuits are so light they float."

Trent laughed and agreed.

After they got over their initial awkwardness, the next hour seemed to fly past as they discussed their ranches, families, and general topics.

Trent said, "I just got a wire that Lilah's nephew, Tim Wells, and his wife and baby are coming to visit. Actually, Tim will be working for us. Rush offered him a job so he could save money for his own place, and we sure could use the help." He tapped his fingers on the table. "You know, I could send him out here to help until your pa and brothers return."

Arizona laughed, "There you go again, trying to order my life. No, Trent, my family will be home any day. And even if they weren't, I wouldn't let you pay for help done on our ranch. You have a big one of your own and need all the hands you can get."

Trent shook his head. "Someday, Arizona, someday…" He didn't finish his sentence.

Arizona cocked an eyebrow. "Someday?"

He studied her eyes. "Nothing." His chair made a muffled sound as he scooted it back across the hard packed dirt floor. "I best be going and let Rush and Lilah know the happy news. I must say, Tim's marriage and a baby come as a big surprise." He got a faraway look. "It'll be nice having a babe around the ranch again.

Since Ivy turned four, she acts like she's all grown up." He reached for his hat on the peg by the door. "I know you don't want to hear this, but stay out of the sun until it cools down a little."

Arizona had an almost overwhelming desire to graze her hand across the stubble on Trent's jaw. She knew he was in his forties, but his tall, lean body, could have passed for that of a man in his early thirties. She also knew he was the topic of conversation between eligible women—and ineligible ones—and wondered if any of the pretty young gals would ever snag him.

With uncharacteristic obedience, she said, "I promise not to work in the garden anymore today."

He looked surprised and then smiled. "Now what brought that on? I expected you to tell me to hobble my lip."

She returned his smile. "It was your charm, sir."

He tipped his hat, guffawed loudly, and stepped outside. "Good day, Arizona."

Chapter 11: Arrival

The soon arrival of Tim and his family sent the household into a frenzy of excitement. Trent watched Pearl and Lilah clean every room in the house—as if they weren't already spotless—and then prepare the largest guest room as if the King and Queen of England were arriving.

On the evening before the big day, Trent gathered with his family around the hearth and listened to the women discuss meal plans. A glance at Rush while Lilah and Pearl playfully argued the merits of beans simmered with ham hocks versus beans with steak chunks, revealed his brother was just as amused as he was.

The day of the arrival became a family affair with Trent and Rush both driving buckboards. Lilah sat beside Rush while Grady O'Granger, a ranch hand that had worked for the Big G since the early days, sat in the bed with Ivy on his lap. Perched across from them was Chad. Pearl rode beside Trent in the other buckboard.

Trent flicked the reins and followed behind Rush. "Giddup horses!" When they reached the main road, Pearl said, "This is just about the most excitement we've had since Rush and Lilah moved to the ranch, not counting the birth of Ivy."

Trent agreed, "You're right about that."

"'Course, if you ever hitched up with a wife, we'd have cause for a month of celebration."

Trent frowned. "Pearl, don't even go there. I'm too old and set in my ways to marry. Besides, I don't think there's a woman in the county who'd have me."

"Oh, pashaw. You're still in yer forties—young enough to have a passel of kids. You're not old 'til you're my age. And there ain't a woman in the county who don't trip over her own feet when yer around. You got that affect on the female population."

Rather than discuss his love life, Trent replied, "Nonsense. As for you being old, you got as much spunk as a twenty year old."

"Now, don't you go tryin' to change the subject, boy. There ain't a trick you and yer brother can pull that I don't know."

Trent sighed. Pearl wasn't going to let the subject drop, so he mentally reclined to listen to her rant.

She continued, "Now, I've said this time and agin, but Arizona Cayson is the woman fer you. And you may not like it, but I got the second sight and saw ya'll kissin' somethin' fierce on top o' the ridge overlookin' the Nueces."

Trent changed his mind about listening to Pearl. "Gawd damn, Pearl, she's in her twenties! I'll say it again; I'm too old for her. She needs a young, strappin' man."

"You are one blind cowboy, Trent Garrett. That woman's been hankerin' fer you to make a move on her since she was sixteen."

Trent inhaled sharply and grunted a warning, but Pearl ignored him.

"And you bein' too old—hogwash! You're more strappin' than most of the young bucks you got hired at the ranch."

"Pearl, let's just drop the subject. Okay?"

"Sure. But droppin' it only spills it and then you got a mess to clean up. 'Course, maybe you need a mess to make you see the light o' day."

Trent ground his jaw and refused to respond. By the time they pulled to the depot in Harper, he'd had an earful. Thankfully, about five miles out, she'd changed her ranting about his love life, to problems with her kitchen and ideas she and Lilah had for an updated and more efficient one. Trent looped the horses' reins to a hitching post and helped Pearl down. What she didn't know was that he and Rush had decided to give the women the kitchen of their dreams.

Rush had already helped Lilah from their buckboard and Grady handed Ivy to him. He swung her in a circle and she squealed with delight. Her infectious giggles started everyone laughing. For a second, Trent thought about his own daughter who would have been a young woman had she lived, and felt sadness for the past. The suggestion planted by Pearl that he could still have children danced across his mind before he quenched it.

Chad asked Rush, "Pa, can I go to the mercantile and buy a candy for me and Ivy?"

"Sure, son. Just be back before the train arrives."

"Yes, sir."

Trent watched the rangy thirteen year old run toward the store. Someday a portion of the Big G would belong to him. Rush had once asked Trent his feelings about an adopted son inheriting a portion of the ranch. Trent had replied, "He's your son and I couldn't be happier that he continue our legacy."

After that, Rush pulled Trent into a hug. "You're a good man and I'm proud to call you my brother."

Rush's words had put a lump the size of El Capitan in Trent's throat. The fact that Rush had left the ranch twenty years earlier spouting hatred toward him, made his words even more special.

A familiar figure leaving the mercantile brought Trent's musings back to the present. Arizona caught sight of his family and waved. His heart did its usual kick and he glanced at Pearl to see an "I-told-you-so" look on her face.

* * *

After placing her order for the dress she'd selected to wear to the yearly hoedown at the Garretts, Arizona turned to see Chad enter the store. Her heart lurched. Was Trent in town? She said goodbye to the store owner and hello to Chad. He replied politely, but his attention was captured by colorful jars of candy. Having raised three younger brothers, Arizona was familiar with that distraction.

Stepping outside the general store, she scanned the area for Trent. Butterflies swamped her stomach when she saw him in front of the depot. Next to him, Pearl and Lilah were talking, and when they saw her they both called and waved her over. She waved back. There was no way she would refuse a chance to be near Trent.

Tucking her receipt into her sorry excuse for a reticule, she smoothed her hand down the skirt of her old calico dress. It had been patched a number of times and had the seams let out over the years to accommodate generous curves. Her bonnet was old and frayed and she suddenly felt like the homeliest woman on earth. She reconsidered visiting with the Garrett family, but, of course, that would be rude, and it wasn't in her nature to knowingly offend, unless, of course, she was pushed beyond tolerance.

Sighing and inhaling deeply, she stepped off the boardwalk and crossed the street.

Trent and Rush removed their hats.

"Howdy, Miss Cayson," said Rush.

Trent said, "Mornin' Arizona. What brings you to town?"

"Just needed to place an order at the mercantile."

Pearl and Lilah came up on either side of her and took turns hugging her. Lilah said with excitement, "My nephew and his wife and baby are arriving today. We had no idea he'd married, so it's a wonderful surprise. You and your family must come for supper tonight. Please say you will."

The happiness radiating from Lilah, a woman of such beauty inside and out that Arizona always admired her with awe, made it impossible to refuse. "My pa and brothers are still out of town but I'd love to come."

Pearl said, "We eat at six. Trent can drive you in your buckboard."

Arizona started to refuse Pearl's directive that Trent accompany her but the whistle of a train interrupted their conversation. Lilah grabbed her husband's arm and he reached around her waist, pulling her close to his body. Chad ran from the mercantile and back to the depot. Ivy clapped her hands and jumped up and down while Pearl and Grady, both short, stood on tiptoes to see over obstacles blocking the line of sight down the tracks. The family's excitement was infectious and Arizona gazed eagerly at the approaching train. The screech of brakes heralded the iron monster's arrival and everyone rushed onto the depot landing to greet the train's occupants.

The conductor was the first to descend. He approached several crew members on the landing, gave instructions, and then reentered the train. Soon passengers began debarking. An elderly man and woman descended first, followed by a young man who turned to help a young woman carrying a blanketed bundle. They looked so happy that Arizona felt a catch in her heart. How she longed for her own husband and children.

The next few minutes became chaotic when Lilah squealed and ran to hug the young man and then encompass his wife and babe. The rest of the folks from Big G surrounded the couple with everyone making them welcome.

Arizona suddenly felt out-of-place. They were family and she wasn't. She started to slip away, but Trent stepped to block her escape. He clasped her elbow and guided her toward the new arrivals. Pearl pulled her forward and made introductions. In the face of such friendliness, Arizona forgot her awkward feelings.

Chapter 12: Bungling No More

For all of Daisy's bravado while living alone and facing life's hardships, meeting Tim's family had her terrified, but when her husband bent, kissed her cheek, and whispered, "You look beautiful," she knew she could do anything with him beside her.

It had only been a week since that fateful day of the tornado, but she would be forever grateful of the outcome. Tim's declaration of love and their subsequent lovemaking had restored her belief in family, home, and happily-ever-after. Whenever she could, she stole kisses from her handsome husband and he seemed more than happy to oblige.

She heard him exclaim, "Aunt Lilah, Uncle Rush, it's good to finally be here! I'd like you to meet my wife, Daisy, and our daughter, June."

The most beautiful woman Daisy had ever seen stepped to enfold her and June in a hug. "Oh, my dear, this is such a wonderful surprise. We had no idea Tim had married and started a family. I shall have to berate my sister for not writing the details."

Tim cleared his throat. "Er, Ma and Pa don't know yet. We've only been married a short time."

Lilah's eyes widened and then she grinned. "How delightful and romantic! I can't wait to hear your story." She giggled and insisted, "Now, I *must* see my grandniece."

Daisy pulled the blanket back and Lilah peeked at the sleeping baby. Standing beside Lilah, Tim's uncle lifted a little girl into his arms and pulled the boy next to him closer so they could see. Everyone exclaimed over June in hushed tones so as not to wake her. Daisy glanced at Tim watching from the sidelines. His big grin was meant just for her. It said louder than words, "I told you my family would love you and June."

In that moment, tears sprang to her eyes. No longer was she bungling through life alone. She had a family again. She tried to blink back tears of joy. Tim was immediately at her side. "Here honey, let me hold the baby for awhile." He lifted June from her arms.

Daisy felt something pressed into her palm and realized it was a hankie. Lilah said, "I need one too," and lifted another one to her own eyes. Together the women blotted their faces while everyone around them talked at once.

While the inexpensive trunk that held her family's meager belongings was unloaded from the train and loaded onto a buckboard, Daisy met the rest of Tim's family. His uncle introduced his daughter, Ivy, and the little girl asked shyly, "Do you think I could hold the baby if I'm very careful?"

Daisy bent to hug her. "You surely can. How about tonight?" The child's eyes lit and she turned to her father to share the news.

Next, Daisy was introduced to Rush and Lilah's son, Chad. Immediately, his sweet smile captured her heart.

An older man and woman stepped forward. The dark-skinned woman said, "Daisy, I'm Pearl, and so happy ya'll are here that we're havin' a feast fit fer royalty tonight. I sure hope ya'll like to eat!"

The older man added, "And ain't no one cooks bettr'n Pearl! Welcome young folks. My name's Grady O'Granger and I been on the ranch jus' 'bout as long as Pearl."

Pearl reached and pulled another woman forward. "And this here is Arizona Cayson. She lives on a ranch not far from the Big G. You both bein' young women, I'll jus' bet you become fast friends."

The woman named Arizona smiled shyly and Daisy knew in her heart they would surely become friends. She clasped Arizona's hand. "Pleased to meet you, ma'am."

Arizona's smile widened. "Please call me Arizona."

"And I'm Daisy."

The last person to be introduced was Trent Garrett. He'd been hanging around in the background until Rush pointed in his direction. "And that big ol' cowboy is my brother Trent. He might look foreboding, but he's got a heart as big as the sky." The tall man stepped forward to welcome Daisy and Tim.

That night, true to her word, Pearl and Lilah cooked up a feast the likes of which Daisy had never seen. Family, friends, and ranch hands gathered around a massive table in a huge dining room while Daisy, Tim, and June were indeed treated like royalty. Daisy could hardly fathom the change in her life over the past two months.

Trent stood and clanged his glass of tea. "I propose a toast."

Everyone lifted their glasses.

Daisy giggled and felt Tim's hand enfold hers under the table.

Trent said, "May this young family that lost all their worldly possessions, but discovered each other in the midst of disaster, rebuild their ranch. May they be blessed with long, healthy lives, many children, and always remember the importance of family." His voice cracked on his last word and Daisy saw him glance at his brother. During the long train ride, Tim had outlined the history of his family and Daisy knew that Trent and Rush had been at odds for many years.

After Trent's toast, a round of toasts proceeded around the table. When the well-wishing reached Arizona, she appeared to hesitate, but then stood and lifted her glass. "I just want to thank the Garretts for inviting me to join them in welcoming the Wells family, and my toast is that Daisy and Tim will always remember the hard times, because they make the good times so much sweeter."

Everyone agreed and finally Tim stood. He lifted his glass, smiled down at Daisy, and said, "I met Daisy when I was eight years old, just after my pa died. She was fun and we became friends. On the day her pa drove me and Ma to town to catch the stagecoach leaving for St. Louey to begin our journey to Oregon, she told me something that ended our friendship."

Around the table there were gasps.

Tim grinned. "She said she'd dreamed we would one day marry. Of course, a mischievous boy doesn't want to hear that and I was a little rude." He laughed. "Actually, I was very rude." Everyone joined Tim's laughter. He stared at his wife. "I don't know if I believe in dreams predicting the future, but I do know that since leaving that day, I've felt compelled to return. I *had* to return. And when I arrived two months ago and Daisy pointed her shotgun at me and told me to get off her land—I fell in love."

The table went silent and Daisy fingered the corners of her eyes. Tim continued staring at his wife. "Daisy, you and June own my heart and I thank God every day your dream came true." He bent and kissed her cheek.

By now, all the women, and even some of the work-hardened men, were brushing away tears.

* * *

Lying in a soft bed in one of Big G's guestrooms, Arizona rehashed all the happenings since she'd met up with the family in town that morning. She loved this family.

She loved Trent.

She heaved a heartfelt sigh. She needed to stop pining for him and give thought to the marriage proposal she'd received from old widower Campbell. He wasn't ancient, maybe sixty, so he could still give her children. He'd even admitted with embarrassment that he wouldn't mind starting a family since his only child, a son, had died of scarlet fever at the age of twenty-five and left no grandchildren. He'd suggested that she, being a young woman, probably wanted children, too. The proposal had been embarrassing for both of them, but Arizona had assured him she would give it serious consideration. They both knew it would be a marriage of convenience—she, for the purpose of having children, and he, to live out his days surrounded by family.

Pushing thoughts of Mr. Campbell aside, Arizona turned onto her side and reflected on her encounters with Trent that day.

Against her protests, he had driven her wagon back to her soddy so she could leave a note for her pa and pack an overnight bag. Grady had replaced Trent in driving the Big G buckboard loaded with Pearl and the Wells family and their trunk. At the crossroad to her ranch, the families in both of Big G's wagons had called cheerful farewells and said they'd see her soon.

By the time she and Trent reached his ranch in the late afternoon, everyone had gathered around the hearth and relaxed on comfortable sofas. They greeted her warmly. Pearl and Lilah were in the kitchen cooking up the promised feast and adamantly refused help. Pearl said guests didn't cook their own meals.

Even after supper, when Arizona tried to help with cleanup, the old woman had waved her away with a plump hand and reiterated, "Guests at Big G don't cook meals or clean dishes." Glancing at Trent, she'd ordered, "You take Arizona for a walk. It's a lovely evening; perfect for strollin' the river."

Trent smiled and offered his arm. "Arizona, may I stroll with you along the river?"

Not wanting to offend Pearl, she nodded, but when they stepped onto the porch, she said, "You really don't have to do this. Pearl was...well, just being Pearl."

Trent trapped Arizona's hand against his elbow when she started to step away. "I was about to suggest a walk myself. Pearl just beat me to it."

Arizona knew he was being polite, but nonetheless, her heart beat faster. She clutched his arm again and they walked toward the river path. When they reached the river, she didn't know what possessed her, but she blurted, "Mr. Campbell proposed to me."

Trent paused midstride and frowned. "Arizona, he's much too old for you. I hope you're not seriously considering it."

His response irritated her and she responded, "I certainly am considering it. I'll be twenty-nine my next birthday and I want a family of my own."

"My God, he's old enough to be your father."

"He's a kind man and would give me a good home."

Trent made an exasperated sound. "Surely, there are young men in the area. Why, new folks move here all the time. Maybe you should wait at least one more year?"

Realizing the futility of her love for Trent, Arizona's heart broke. Deep down, she knew that by announcing Mr. Campbell's proposal, she had hoped to make him a tiny bit jealous. Obviously, he wasn't. Before she could reconsider what she was about to do, she stepped in front of him, stood on tiptoe, reached her arms to encircle his neck, and mashed her lips against his. She was determined to know what kissing Trent was like. He didn't move.

He still didn't move when she sighed into his mouth. Guided by instinct, she gentled the kiss and hoped she was doing it right. This was her first kiss. She touched her tongue to his lips.

After that, the man ignited like a spark on dry hay. His arms encircled her and pulled her so close they were like one body. Big hands roamed her back before settling on her waist, while his mouth did things to hers that had her gasping. When he reached lower onto her posterior, she groaned and said, "I love you, Trent. I would make you a good wife."

He went perfectly still, inhaled deeply, and placed his hands on her shoulders to set her away from him. With lips still moist from her kisses, he said, "I'm not the man for you, Arizona. I'm not marriage material. I loved and lost years ago. I'm sure you've heard the rumors about me and Rush's first wife." He stared hard into her eyes. "The rumors are true. When Katy died, I swore I'd never entangle myself with another woman."

Arizona shook her head. "Then I feel sorry for you. We could be happy and raise a beautiful family. You would have children to carry on your legacy."

With a steely gaze, he replied, "Rush's children will carry on the legacy. I'll never marry."

Smiling sadly, but with a voice just as resolute, she said, "Then you're a fool."

After that, she'd turned and followed the trail back to the house.

Chapter 13: Learning from the Best

Tim swung the circle of rope over his head and lassoed a wayward calf. Dismounting, he checked the little bugger for injuries, decided there were none, and then pointed him in the right direction, slapping his flank after removing the rope. He yelled, "He's fine."

The calf's mother, surrounded by Trent and Rush on horseback, was none to happy about being separated from her baby and vocalized her frustration until she was released. The reunited mother and calf rushed toward the safety of the herd.

Trent said, "You're pretty good with that rope. As a matter-of-fact, you're a helluva good ranch hand."

Rush said, "I couldn't agree more."

"Thanks. Coming from both of you, that means a lot."

The men rounded up a few more strays and then decided to call it a day as the sun bowed low on the horizon. Tim said as they trotted toward home, "Ya'll have a beautiful spread and I've learned a lot this past month. I can't wait to get my own place going again and implement some new practices. I think I'll try raising a few head of cattle."

Rush said, "It's unfortunate there wasn't a single building left standing after the tornado."

"That's true, but there's timber nearby, a good well, and fertile land. Me and Daisy have a plan for getting the place rebuilt when we return." Thoughts of Daisy made Tim grin and he turned his head so he wouldn't look like a lovesick cowboy to these two work-roughened men. Of course, seeing how crazy Rush was over Lilah, he knew the man would understand. As for Trent, Tim wondered if he had a hankering for Miz Arizona. Since the night of the celebration he'd seen her only once, and that had been when he'd ridden in the buckboard with Trent to deliver grain sacks to her ranch. Seems the families leasing Big G land got a better deal buying from Trent and Rush than the grainery in town.

At the time, he'd met her pa and two of her brothers, the third one having gone off on his own a few months previous. Her pa was a short, sturdily built man with a lined face and stern expression. Apparently, he was a man of few words because he'd rudely walked away after introductions. Arizona had sighed, shook her head, and said, "Sorry about that, Tim. He's an ornery old cuss and he'll get a piece of my mind later." Then she'd stared hard at Trent. "He's a lot like another cowboy I know." Her meaning had come across loud and clear and Trent had tipped his hat. "We'll deliver another load in a week. Good day, Arizona." He'd then called a farewell to her brothers who were moving the grain sacks into the barn, "See ya'll later." The young men had waved and gone back to work.

Now, pausing their horses on the rise above the ranch that afforded a view of the Nueces river, Rush said, "Two more days and this place will be crowded with folks from all over the county."

Trent agreed, "Yep. And I got a feelin' it's gonna be the biggest hoedown yet."

Rush laughed. "You got that right. Everyone and his cousin are wantin' to make Tim's and Daisy's acquaintance." He glanced at Tim. "The whole county has heard how you traveled the Oregon Trail, so you best be ready to answer a thousand questions. Some of these folk have never even been to the next county so they love a good adventure tale."

Tim steadied the reins of his horse when he danced sideways. "Then I'll reminisce my best stories with them—especially the one about the baby in the quicksand."

Trent shook his head. "I've heard that one and it gives me the willies."

Tim laughed. "I'll make sure to ham it up for the locals, but the fact is, it was a serious situation. If my ma hadn't been fast thinking and kept us afloat the few minutes needed for Cooper to arrive, that babe and I would have been sucked under."

Rush said, "I know how serious quicksand is. I once had a helluva time pulling a man out with a rope. He'd escaped from the local jail and swore he'd turn himself in if I'd save him from that horrible death. Heck, I would have saved him anyway, but he didn't know that. He was true to his word, though, and came peaceful with me.

"But, changing the subject, our women have been sewing up a storm. Lilah refuses to let me see the dress she made for the hoedown. How about Daisy, have you seen her dress?"

Tim chuckled, "Nope. She's not even keeping it in the bedroom. Said she doesn't want me to peek."

Rush started down the rise. "Lilah could wear a flour sack and I'd still think she was the most beautiful woman ever born."

Tim smiled. "I feel the same way about Daisy."

* * *

Trent listened to the banter between Rush and Tim and stifled his envy. Since Arizona had kissed him at the river and he'd rejected her marriage proposal, he'd been battling emotions as big as the sky. So far, he hadn't heard any rumors about her accepting Mr. Campbell's proposal and he hoped to hell she'd turned him down.

Chapter 14: Helluva Hoedown

Daisy twirled before Tim in the dress Lilah had designed. The woman was a fabulous seamstress and had confided that before she met and married Rush, she had intended to open her own dress shop in New Orleans. Daisy had noticed all the fine clothing that Pearl, Lilah, and the children wore and now she understood. When Lilah had said she wanted to sew a beautiful dress for Daisy, she had immediately protested.

"Oh, no, Lilah, you must sew it for yourself."

Lilah waved her protest aside. "I'll do no such thing. Besides," she giggled, "I already did. I sewed gowns for me and Pearl and Ivy weeks ago. No, honey, this is my gift to you." She winked. "And I'm going to make a matching dress for June. Ivy has one like mine. She loves to dress like her ma. I know June is too young to know, but you can save the dress and show her someday."

Daisy looked shyly away. "I-I can't accept because I haven't any money for material."

Lilah frowned and then grinned. "Come with me, I want to show you something."

Following Lilah into her and Rush's bedroom, Daisy gasped at the elegance of it. Beautiful blue silks of many shades flowed over the one window and matched the colors of the coverlet on the bed. Sky blue throw rugs dotted the oak floor. Polished mahogany furniture gleamed beneath silks of lavender.

Daisy held her hand over her heart. "I've never seen such a beautiful room."

Lilah smiled sweetly. "The way I figure it, the room you share with your husband should be the grandest of all."

When Daisy thought about that, she had to agree. Maybe someday she and Tim would have a beautiful bedroom mirroring their beautiful lives.

Lilah paused before a door at the back of the room, and grinned. "This room was intended to be a small office when Rush's mother designed it. She was a forward thinking woman when it came to architecture." Lilah opened the door and motioned Daisy forward. Daisy stepped inside and again gasped. Lilah said, "Now it's the sewing room I always wanted. I design and sew dresses and make fancy hats in here. There's a dress shop in town that sells my creations."

Daisy turned in a room cluttered with fabric and partially draped body forms. A wall of fabric bolts, more than any she'd seen in a mercantile, was stacked almost to the ceiling. Every shade, print, and texture teased her eyes—apple green and cherry red cottons, lemon yellow linen, pristine white and midnight black satins, coffee brown wool, delicate tulles and lace, floral prints, and everything in between. The center of the room boasted a shiny Singer sewing machine, the fanciest Daisy had ever seen. She didn't know what to say.

Lilah reached for a sketch pad and started outlining a gown. Within the hour, Daisy was staring at the drawing of a dress she had only fantasized about.

Now she twirled in front of Tim in the lavender taffeta gown with its small, but fashionable bustle, puffed sleeves, and scooped neckline revealing a hint of cleavage. June lay on the bed cooing. Daisy shyly asked, "Do you like my surprise?"

Tim looked dumfounded. "Darlin' you're so beautiful you take my breath away."

At his sweet words, Daisy ran and threw her arms around his neck. "I love you so much!" After that there was so much kissing and caressing that Daisy had to finally break away. "Goodness Tim, if we don't go now, I fear we shall never get there."

Tim continued nuzzling her ear. "After the hoedown, I'm going to remove that dress one inch at a time."

Daisy's heart jumped and she almost wanted to forget the dance. Giggling, she stole one last kiss and then stepped to lift the blanket covering June. "Look, Tim."

Tim glanced at June and his face lit with a grin that warmed Daisy's heart. She laughed. "The matching dress was Lilah's idea. Isn't it wonderful!"

Tim picked June up and kissed her cheek. The baby grinned and reached her chubby hand to grab a handful of his hair. "Oh, Daisy, you and June are my very heart." He lifted love filled eyes to Daisy's.

Remembering the dark and lonely days of her life, she reached to caress her husband's cheek. As Arizona had said, dark days only made the good times so much sweeter.

* * *

Trent lost count of how many times he'd tried to get his string tie to hang straight. Finally, he gave up and accepted that it was going to be cockeyed. He fastened the buttons of his black silk vest embroidered with swirling blue threads, and pulled on his matching frock coat. There was something to be said about having a resident seamstress. He'd never met a woman who enjoyed sewing as much as Lilah. And with the way Pearl loved to cook, he figured the household was just about perfect. Well, perfect except for the loneliness that always gnawed at his heart. He'd come to accept it over the years, but now, seeing the happiness his brother and nephew had found with their families, his loneliness felt magnified.

Positioning his Stetson and giving one last swipe to a scuff on his dress boots, he headed toward the living room where everyone had agreed to meet. Tim and Daisy were already there and making eyes at each other. Trent almost laughed aloud at their young love. Tim saw him enter and tore his eyes away from Daisy.

Trent said, "Daisy, you look beautiful!" He glanced sideways at Tim, "And you clean up pretty good yourself, young man."

Tim laughed. "I must say, Trent, you're wearin' just about the fanciest suit I've ever seen."

"You just wait. Your turn's a-comin'. Lilah would sew clothes for the hounds if she could."

A voice from the hallway entrance chuckled. "As a matter-of-fact, I do have an idea for dog coats when the weather turns cold."

Everyone in the room except Rush stood agape at her words. He said matter-of-factly, "And she's not kidding. I saw the drawing myself." He started laughing and the family joined in. Rush held Lilah's elbow as they entered the room. As always, the woman was one of the most stunning Trent had ever laid eyes on. Rush had confided to Trent shortly after his return to the ranch that Lilah had once been a courtesan. Of course, seeing the happiness she brought his brother, Trent could have cared less. After the heartache he'd caused by loving his brother's first wife, he'd welcomed a second chance with him and opened his arms to anyone who made Rush happy—and Lilah made him *very* happy.

Pearl and Ivy entered the room and Ivy ran to her mother. "See Mama, Pearl made my hair real pretty." Lilah bent and hugged her daughter. "You look like a princess." Ivy twirled in her dress. "I look just like you, Mama."

Rush reached and scooped his daughter up. I'm taking two princesses to the dance."

Ivy giggled. "Papa, put me down. You'll wrinkle my dress."

Chad walked into the room and everyone's attention focused on him. He looked elegant in a brown suit that also had a vest with fancy embroidery. He pulled at his collar. Lilah laughed, "Son, you'll be back in your grubs tomorrow. But tonight, I think every young girl won't be able to keep her eyes off you."

Chad stretched his collar some more. "Aw, Ma, don't say things like that."

The family was complete except for Grady who wasn't really family, although everyone thought of him as such.

Rush said, "People have already begun to arrive and Grady and the hands have been escorting them to the barn. Is everyone ready?"

Pearl placed her hand in the crook of Trent's arm and said, "You can escort me. When we get to the barn, you can find Arizona."

Trent frowned, but it didn't keep her from saying, "And you be sure to dance with her, hear?"

Before he could reply, she was tugging him toward the front door and he decided this year's gathering was going to be one helluva hoedown!

* * *

Arizona clasped her hands so tightly in her lap her knuckles turned white. Her pa pulled their old buckboard to the first free spot he could find way out past the barn at the Big G. It looked like the whole county and even the next one, had shown up for the festivity. Arizona's brothers jumped off the bed and waited for the buckboard to stop. Her pa alighted, told Tad to help his sister down, gave a back-handed wave, and headed toward the barn, already reaching for the flask in his pocket.

Arizona sighed and Tad said, "He'll be soppin' drunk by the time we leave."

Her other brother, Slim, responded, "If Ma was here, she wouldn't believe the man he's become."

Tad snorted, "Hell, it's time he got over her death. Don't ya think sixteen years is long enough."

Arizona interrupted, "Well, I, for one, am not going to let Pa ruin my night. See ya'll later."

She'd only taken one step when Tad said, "Hey, Arizona…"

She turned and watched her baby brother grin, "You sure look pretty."

Slim, with his characteristic impatience, said, "Come on Tad, stop lollygaggin' and help me with these horses." He looked at Arizona and winked. "Yeah, you clean up nice, sis."

Arizona laughed, waved, and practically skipped to the barn entrance. She almost felt pretty in her new dress. Well, at least her dress was pretty. The glazed muslin was such a beautiful shade of lavender it had taken her breath away. Arriving only two days earlier, she had been sweating the fact that it might not come in time for the hoedown.

Smoothing her hands down the cinched waist and then the full skirt, she willed her racing heart to slow. At the entrance, she paused before stepping into a room radiating light from multiple lanterns that changed an ordinary barn into something magical.

He heart beat faster. Would Trent like her dress?

She was jostled by a young boy chasing Ivy. She recognized the blacksmith's son. He said, "Sorry, Miz Arizona." He started to turn away, but stopped. "That sure is a pretty dress."

Happiness flooded her. "Thank you, Georgie."

As she had done all her life, Arizona immediately skirted to the side of the room so as to be unobtrusive. A few people greeted her and she responded politely. Mostly, she just wanted to find a spot to watch the happenings and imagine what it would be like to have an adoring husband and children. She located a place beside some bales of hay and grinned at old Mr. and Mrs. Whippendell on the dance floor kicking up their feet to a lively tune. They'd always been the best dancers in the community and loved to teach anyone who wanted to learn.

After a few minutes, her gaze wandered to the far side of the huge barn and her breath whooshed from her body. Daisy stood beside her husband in the most beautiful gown Arizona had ever clapped eyes on. The color was identical to Arizona's dress and it also had a fitted waist and wide skirt, but in a much more fashionable style—like a big city gown.

Arizona watched Lilah and Rush step beside Daisy. Not only was Lilah the most beautiful woman imaginable, she was also the sweetest. Rush bent to his wife's ear and said something before clasping her hand and leading her to the dance floor. They looked like they'd stepped from the pages of the gothic romance Arizona kept hidden beneath her mattress. She sighed.

A voice from behind startled her and made her heart gallop. Trent said, "You look lovely, Arizona. I saw you enter the barn. Why are you hiding behind the hay? You should be dancing with the young gents."

She knew Trent was trying to force her to mingle with younger men after the conversation they'd had about Mr. Campbell, and it instantly got her hackles up. She turned and said, "I'm looking for Mr. Campbell."

Her response drew a reaction that surprised her. For a fleeting moment, he looked jealous. She lifted her chin. "You look nice, yourself," she said stiffly.

Unexpectedly, he clasped her elbow. "May I have this dance?" He didn't lead her toward the dance floor until she barely nodded.

The musicians had switched to a slower song after a boot stomping one and Trent moved his hand from Arizona's arm to encircle her waist. His other hand held hers and he pulled her closer than decorum would dictate. For an instant, she resisted, but when she inhaled his scent of fresh air and peppermint, she couldn't stop herself from melting into his arms. They danced on the fringes of the crowd, and even while she wished they were alone, she was grateful they weren't. She would make a fool of herself…again."

The music ended but Trent kept dancing. The fiddlers started a lively tune and he stepped backward. Before he could say anything, one of his young hired hands stepped forward. "Miz Arizona, I don't 'spose you'd like to dance with me, would ya?"

Arizona looked at Chet, a cowboy Trent sometimes sent to deliver grain to her ranch, and smiled. He had orange hair and enough freckles to make his skin the same color. He also looked like he'd barely worked up the courage to ask her to dance. "I'd love to dance with you, Chet."

Chet grinned so big that Arizona could see his back teeth. Trent handed her over. "You two have fun." The look he gave her said everything. *Here's a man your age.*

Arizona could feel steam coming off her head, but she smiled and stepped into Chet's arms. She said cheerily, "You haven't seen Mr. Campbell around, have you? There's something I need to discuss with him." She sent Trent a pointed look when her dance partner twirled her. He merely shook his head.

Although Trent didn't ask her to dance again, Arizona was always aware of him and often caught him watching her. She received several compliments on her dress and Daisy and Lilah told her how pretty she looked. Daisy reached for her hand. "Look, our dresses are almost the same. Don't you love this color? I've never worn anything so fine. I feel like a princess."

Arizona squeezed her hand. "And you look like one, too. As a matter of fact, your husband looks like a prince."

Daisy giggled. "Some days I have to pinch myself. Three months ago I was in the worst situation you can imagine. I had a babe and no husband and a farm to run with no help. Then–" she got a dreamy look, "Tim showed up and I pulled my shotgun on him."

Arizona laughed. "I almost fell on the floor when he told us the story at your welcoming supper."

Daisy smiled. "I demanded he leave, but he wouldn't. He took up residence in the barn and worked my farm. Then, the tornado came and we lost everything. It was the best day of my life."

Arizona said, "Daisy, you're a woman after my own heart. I keep trying to find the silver lining in the midst of heartbreak, and you actually did find it. I'm so happy for you."

Daisy searched Arizona's face. "You have heartache?"

Arizona berated herself for saying too much. In response, she just said, "Sometimes."

"You know, you can talk to me about anything. I think we have a lot in common and I'd love to be your friend."

Arizona felt a lump in her throat. "I think we already are."

Chapter 15: Overnight

Around midnight, the crowd began to thin as fathers and mothers loaded their children onto wagons, buckboards and buggies, and called weary, but happy, goodbyes. The Garretts had welcomed anyone wanting to spend the night and a few lucky families were able to snag the extra guestrooms. The others bedded down in the barn in areas prepared with straw and blankets.

Arizona went in search of her pa and brothers. Tad stormed toward her and angrily said, "Pa's so drunk he took the buckboard and left without us. One of the Gilley children saw him leave over an hour ago. Sheeit, if he weren't our pa I'd beat the devil out of him."

Arizona almost echoed his sentiment, but refrained when she saw Trent approaching. The last thing she wanted was for him to find out and feel sorry for her. Maybe a neighbor would lend her a horse and she could return with the buckboard for her brothers.

When Trent reached them he was already aware that the elder Mr. Cayson had left. "Tad, Slim, there's room for ya'll to bed down with the hands. Arizona, you can stay with Pearl. She insists you share her room."

"I'll do no such thing. Just let me borrow one of your horses. My brothers can stay and I'll bring the buckboard back in the morning."

Trent's stance stiffened. "Absolutely not! It's not safe for a woman to go traipsin' across the countryside in the dead of night."

"Trent, I know this territory like the back of my hand. Just loan me a horse and–"

"Forget it, Arizona. Pearl's waiting for you in the kitchen." He turned and stalked away before she could retort.

Tad said with a touch of exasperation, "I sure wish the two of you would stop squabbling and just admit your feelings for each other."

Arizona looked sharply at him and was about to deny his observation, but he said, "I'm beat. I'll find Slim and let him know what's going on. Go to bed, sis."

Arizona watched her brother walk toward the barn and wanted to stomp her foot. She hated having her life controlled and dictated by another. If it wasn't her father, it was her brothers. She should just marry old man Campbell. At least then she would be mistress of her own home and he was so old he'd probably let her do whatever she wanted. Sighing she walked toward the house.

In the kitchen, Pearl greeted her warmly and didn't mention anything about Arizona's pa being the reason for her predicament. Pearl's bedroom was lovely and her bed big enough for two. While they stared at the darkened ceiling, she told Arizona about the early years of Big G Ranch and how Trent and Rush's parents had saved her from the slavers and hid her for years, and even taught her how to read and write. Pearl didn't focus on her plight; she turned the conversation toward the Garretts and they laughed over the boyish antics of Trent and Rush before their mother died. After her death, Pearl spoke of the sadness that had enveloped the house. "But sadness can only last for so long if you've a mind to go on with your life. The boys' pa decided laughter needed to return to Big G and went all out raisin' them children. The place come alive agin."

Pearl sighed and Arizona wasn't sure if she would continue her story. A couple of minutes passed and then she said, "Everything was good until the senior Mr. Garrett died in a cattle accident. I tried to warn him 'bout my second sight seein' somethin' terrible, but he didn't b'lieve in stuff like that. The boys did, though, and rode out with him that day. Even so, they couldn't stop his horse from throwin' him when a rattler spooked it. His head landed on a rock and he died instantly."

Arizona said, "I heard about the accident, but I never knew exactly what happened. That's so sad."

Pearl reached in the dark and patted Arizona's arm. "Yep, sad times was back. As if that wasn't bad enough, six months later, Rush's wife died. The brothers almost killed each other over Katy." She heaved a heavy sigh. "I 'spose you know why. Hell, the whole county does. Rush loved Katy and so did Trent, and she died birthin' Trent's babe." Pearl made a tiny crying sound.

Arizona said, "You don't have to talk about it."

"Honey, I'm not one to gossip. The only reason I'm tellin' you is 'cause I want you to understand Trent. He feels things real deep. He's packed his guilt 'round for over twenty-five years; even after him and Rush mended the breach. I still see it in his eyes. Oh, don't git me wrong, there's lotsa' joy here since Rush returned with Lilah and Chad. It was like a miracle. And after Ivy was born, there was more joy."

Arizona smiled in the dark. "And now Tim and Daisy are here with their baby."

"Yep. All the happiness makes my heart sing…well, almost. The only thing keepin' this place from bein' heaven on earth is Trent. He needs a wife and youngins', but he's got some crazy notion he's not meant to have his own family."

Arizona blinked back tears. "I hope he finds someone."

Pearl chuckled. "He already has; jus' won't admit to it."

Arizona sniffed and swiped her eyes.

"It's you, Arizona, right in his own backyard fer years. You and him are meant to be husband and wife."

"Oh, no, Pearl, he doesn't see me like that." Arizona's tears wouldn't stop.

"I beg to disagree. He can't take his eyes off you and whenever I bring your name up, he gets madder'n a scalded cat. That's a sure sign o' love. You jus' hang in there a bit longer; my second sight tells me he's 'bout to have a wake-up call. Sure wish I knew more, but that's the way the sight works. Never gives the whole picture."

Arizona remained silent because she knew arguing would be useless. Soon, Pearl was lightly snoring and Arizona turned onto her side. She should marry old Mr. Campbell and put an end to her constant yearning. If she was married, she'd have to stop waiting for something to happen between her and Trent.

Arizona woke before daylight and slipped from under the covers. Pearl still snored. Quietly donning her new dress she fingered the pretty color. In no way was it as extravagant as Daisy's had been, but the similarity was unmistakable.

Leaving Pearl's room, she walked toward the front of the house and was surprised to find Daisy already up with June. The young mother looked up from rocking her child. "Mornin' Arizona. You're up early. You should still be sleepin' after such a late night."

"I always rise early. Don't need much sleep." She walked to sit beside Daisy so she could coo at the baby.

Daisy asked, "You want to hold her?"

"I'd love to."

For several minutes the new friends laughed over funny happenings from the previous night. Soon, the sun began lighting the windows and Daisy said, "Sometimes I take June outside at dawn. I want her to see how pretty everything is. Would you like to join us?"

"Oh, yes."

Daisy pointed to a peg by the door. "You can wear my bonnet, the blue one. I'm going to wake Tim and see if he wants to join us. You can take June outside now, if you want, and I'll join you in a few minutes."

"Okay, I'll meet you by the tree line." Daisy held June while Arizona tied the strings of the bonnet.

Daisy grinned and blushed. "Give me a few minutes. My husband is sometimes slow to get out of bed."

Chapter 16: Morning Walk

Arizona cuddled June to her breast and stepped outside into a brisk morning. Except for Grady O'Granger walking across the yard with his unusual gait, the ranch was quiet. Arizona waved and he waved back.

Chad's dog trotted up. "Hello, Tex. You're up early," she said playfully. Tex wagged his tail and circled her happily. Soon, however, his attention was distracted by a cat running behind the barn and he rushed to investigate.

Walking toward the river trail Arizona made baby talk with June. Now wide awake, the child turned her head to see everything. At the trail's entrance, Arizona paused and looked back toward the ranch. "Your ma and pa will be here soon. Maybe we'll all walk to the river? Would you like that, sweetheart?"

June gurgled and grinned. Her toothless smile was endearing and Arizona kissed her cheek. "Oh, look, baby girl." She turned June to see two squirrels running up and down a tree trunk. "Let's see if we can get closer." She tiptoed down the trail and toward the oak until the surprised squirrels jumped to the ground and darted away. June's irresistible laughter sent happiness into Arizona's heart.

A noise distracted her and she turned, thinking that Tex had found them again. At first, she was confused, and then she was terrified. A man wearing a bandana over his mouth and with his hat pulled low, sat atop a bay horse. Two other cowboys on horses and also wearing bandanas, watched from a distance. The man said, "Scream, and you and your babe are dead." Then he called to the others, "I got her!"

Arizona started to run, but the cowboy jumped to the ground, grabbed her by the waist, and lifted her sidesaddle onto his horse. Mounting quickly behind her, he reined his steed away from the river trail. Arizona's gut instinct suddenly told her these men wouldn't go to so much trouble just to kill her or June. She screamed at the top of her lungs and kept screaming until the man reached and punched her hard across the face.

In a fog, she heard the kidnapper shout, "I'll ride out. You stay and hold 'em off, like we planned. We'll meet up at the hideout."

The baby wailed and it was all Arizona could do to keep from blacking out and losing her hold on June.

* * *

Trent had just stepped into the living room and was greeting Daisy and Tim when Grady O'Granger burst through the door. At the same time, wearing only her nightgown, Pearl ran barefooted into the room. She yelled, "I jus' got the second sight!"

Grady shouted, "I saw Arizona with the babe headin' toward the river. Not long after that I heard 'em yellin'!"

Daisy rushed toward the door. "Arizona was taking June for a walk!"

Before Daisy reached the tiled entrance, Trent and Tim were past her and reaching for their revolvers in their gun belts hanging from hooks. Tim ordered, "Pearl, hold my wife back."

Trent heard Daisy's protests and Pearl's words meant to comfort as he and Tim rushed outside. By the time they reached the trailhead, Rush caught up with them. With his revolver tucked under his armpit he was still fastening his pants over his long johns. "What the hell's going on?" he shouted.

Trent replied, "Beats me." He ordered Grady, "Stay behind the tree line.

"Yes, sir."

Inside the trees, Trent pointed to the tracks of a horse.

Rush bent for a closer look. "There's been a scuffle." He touched an indentation. "That's a woman's shoe."

Tim said, "Oh, God, surely he wouldn't have followed us here."

Trent looked questioningly at Tim, whose face had turned ashen.

Tim said quickly, "June's natural father died recently and his pa wanted Daisy to come live at his ranch so he could raise June. He threatened to take her away from Daisy."

Trent looked at Rush. "I'll order the men to saddle horses."

Suddenly, a shot rang out and ricocheted off a rock, barely missing Rush. "What the hell!"

Another shot blasted the air.

Tim said, "Shit on a shingle! I've been hit!"

Trent was already lunging for the young man to pull him behind a tree.

Grady yelled, "Hold on, boys! Help's a comin'!"

Tim's wound spurted blood and Trent placed his hand over it to stop the bleeding. He called out, "Rush, I've got to get Tim back to the house. I'm tossin' our guns your way."

Behind another tree, Rush yelled, "And I'll put them to good use."

Trent shouted, "Grady, we need a distraction. Let all the horses loose!"

"Yes, sir!"

Soon horses ran amuck and gun fire was exchanged between the ranch hands, the outlaws, and Rush. Trent lifted Tim over his shoulder and ran for all he was worth, darting in and out of the horses. He finally made it to the front porch. As soon as he hit the top step, the door was pushed open by Pearl and he rushed inside.

In the midst of gunfire and Daisy's crying, Pearl said calmly, "Bring him to my room." She looked at Daisy. "Go heat some water."

Daisy's shocked expression was suddenly replaced by resolve and she ran toward the kitchen.

Pearl and Lilah stood behind Trent as he lowered Tim to the bed. Barely conscious, the young man rasped, "Where's Daisy?"

Pearl smoothed her hand across his brow. "She'll be right here, son. Now, I gotta look at that wound." She reached inside her nightstand and pulled out scissors. Lilah helped her remove Tim's shirt. The bleeding wasn't as bad as before, but the wound looked serious.

Tim groaned. "Tell Daisy I'm sorry I wasn't more diligent. Tell her I love her." He reached and grasped Trent's shirt sleeve. Between ragged breaths, he rasped, "You have to find June." He lost consciousness.

Trent stepped away from the women. "I've got to go back." He heard Daisy sob from the doorway. Pearl directed her to set the pot of hot water on the nightstand. After she obeyed, she moved to the opposite side of the bed and knelt beside her husband. "Don't you die on me, Timmy Wells. Do you hear me? Don't you die!" Her voice rose in volume until the last sentence was a shout.

Without looking up, Pearl said, "Trent, you go do what you gotta do. Me and Daisy and Lilah will take care of Tim."

He left the room but her words carried down the hall. "And don't git yerself shot or killed, ya hear?"

"Yes, ma'am," he called as he rushed to his room and grabbed his rifle.

Running through the kitchen, he cracked the side door and peered outside. "Good," he whispered.

A few horses had stayed nearby. Just inside the trees Venus was munching grass. Since the shooting was taking place in front of the ranch, he decided to chance running and using the horses as cover. Lifting his eyes heavenward, even though he wasn't a religious man, he said a silent prayer before hunching low and bounding forward. He reached the horses, slapped one and ran alongside it until it outran him. He was almost to the trees when a bullet sang past his ear. Another slammed into the dirt in front of him.

Dammit! He zigzagged—ten feet to go. No more shots rang out and he figured the kidnappers were reloading. He darted behind the closest mesquite tree. His horse had moved further inside the tree line and lazily lifted her head, seemingly more concerned with eating than the sound of gun blasts. The gunfire started up again.

Moving from tree to tree, Trent eased toward her. "Venus, I need your help. We've got some bad hombres to catch." He whistled and she lifted and tossed her head and started toward him. Reaching for Venus's mane, he hoisted himself bareback onto her. Bending to her ear, he said, "You know what to do." He kicked her flank. The horse obeyed without question and Trent led her toward the river, intending to circle and come up behind the outlaws.

All gun fire suddenly ceased. Trent said, "Whoa, girl," and waited. He heard his men calling out to one another and edged his horse back toward the ranch. A couple of hands who had ventured beyond the trees, ran into the open. One of them called, "They're gone!"

Trent watched Rush run toward the ranch, zigzagging to confuse any attackers, but no shots rang out. He reached the porch and darted inside.

Galloping back toward the kitchen door, Trent dismounted and yelled to Grady who was limping toward him. "Saddle Venus and tell the men to gather the horses. I need five volunteers to make up a posse. You come too, Grady. You're the best tracker there is. Also, send someone to Harper to let the sheriff know what's happened."

"Yes sir." Grady turned and hurried as fast as his bum leg would allow.

Slim and Tad rushed toward him. Tad said, "What the hell is going on? We heard gunfire and then your foreman told us to stay with the folks in the barn to make sure they laid low and no one walked outside."

Trent paused mid-stride. "Your sister and the Wells' baby were kidnapped by unknown assailants."

Both Tad and Slim looked incredulous and then Slim burst into a round of profanities.

Trent started walking again, but called back, "If ya'll want to join up with the posse, tell Grady to get you lined out with horses."

As soon as Trent stepped inside the kitchen he was met by Rush.

Rush said, "You okay?"

"Yeah. I was circling on Venus intending to come up from behind when the firing stopped. Grady's gathering a posse."

"Good. How's Tim?"

Trent exhaled sharply. "He's shot pretty bad. Don't know if the bullet is still in him. Pearl and Lilah were working on him when I left." Glancing past Rush, he saw Chad and Ivy standing in the kitchen entrance holding hands. He motioned with his head and Rush turned around.

Hastening toward his children, Rush said, "Son, I want you to take your sister to her room and stay with her. Help her get dressed. I'll come say goodbye before I leave."

Chad swallowed. "Yes, sir."

Enfolding his children in a hug, he reassured them, "Everything's going to be all right. Go on now."

Trent and Rush followed the children from the kitchen. Trent quietly opened Pearl's door. On one side of the bed Pearl and Lilah worked on Tim while Daisy still knelt on the opposite side, soothing his forehead with a damp cloth. His eyes were closed and his skin pasty looking.

Lilah turned at the sound of the door opening and her red-rimmed eyes and serious expression didn't bode well. Pearl said without looking up, "The bullet's lodged in his side, under a rib. I gots to git it out. He's gonna need laudanum and a strong man to hold him down."

Trent looked at Rush. "I'll do it."

Rush nodded.

Pearl advised, "Gimme ten minutes to dose him and git him ready."

Trent puffed a breath. "I'll be back." He motioned Rush outside the room. When they stepped into the hallway, he said, "I don't know how long this will take, but we need to be on the trail of those outlaws."

Rush said, "If you're still helping Pearl by the time the men are ready, I'll lead them out and you can catch up."

"Sounds good."

Ten minutes later, Trent stood beside Pearl and Lilah while Daisy continued to smooth a cloth over Tim's sweat-beaded forehead.

Trent had complete faith in Pearl's doctoring skills. From her childhood, she had dealt with various life-threatening accidents—first on a plantation, and later with a band of runaway slaves. After being brought to Big G, she'd nursed more than one family member or ranch hand. Often, she was called upon by neighbors for her expertise.

Pearl nodded and he placed his hands on Tim's shoulders. The ladies had already tied his hands and feet to the bed frame. Daisy released a soft sob and then said quickly, "I'm sorry. I'm sorry. I can do this."

Pearl said, "Honey, I'd tell ya to leave, but I knows it won't do no good." Staring at Trent, she said, "Let's git this done."

For the next several minutes, amidst moans and then yells from Tim, she enlarged the wound, searched for the bullet, retrieved it, and then doused the opening with alcohol. By the time she'd finished, Tim had lost consciousness again.

Although tears dripped from Lilah's and Daisy's cheeks, both women did what was required of them with grit and fortitude.

In the midst of the operation, Rush had stuck his head back in. "We're leaving. And we won't return until we've rescued June and Arizona."

Trent said, "I'll catch up."

Lilah said without taking her gaze off Tim while she sponged blood so Pearl could see, "I love you, Rush. Please come back to me."

"That I will, darlin'."

Now, with Pearl sewing the wound shut, Trent exited to the water closet and splashed himself. So far, he hadn't allowed himself to dwell on the reality that Arizona was in the hands of outlaws. He looked at himself in the mirror and saw the resolve in his eyes. If they hurt her, he'd personally kill them.

Chapter 17: Weak Eyes

Arizona held June tightly to her bosom. She had no understanding as to why she and the baby had been abducted, except that she'd heard rumors of women being forced into bordellos and babies sold on the black market.

While her kidnapper charged past trees and shrubs, she heard gunfire and prayed no one from the Big G got hurt. June continued screaming and she did her best to comfort the child, although it was impossible with the galloping horse. Her cheek ached from being punched and felt swollen.

The outlaw seemed to know where he was going because he skirted known trails and kept his horse moving southward. After maybe five hours, he guided his bay into a canyon. An hour later, he entered a narrow gap between large outcroppings of boulders. Soon, Arizona was lost in the maze. June had exhausted herself crying and now slept. The babe would wake soon and be hungry.

The outlaw rounded another outcropping and approached a shack. He dismounted and reached toward Arizona. None too gently, he grabbed her waist and hauled her off the horse. June whimpered, but did not wake up.

He commanded, "Go in the cabin."

Without questioning his order, she entered the shabby hut. It was tiny and the only furniture was a warped plank table and a couple of hand-hewn chairs. She sat in the sturdiest appearing chair, not even wiping the dust off. She didn't want to wake June.

Through the open doorway, she saw the cowboy tending his horse. For the next hour she planned different strategies for escape.

In the afternoon, other men joined them and she assumed they were the same outlaws from that morning. She watched the man who had brought her to the cabin walk toward them and heard him say, "It's about time."

"Hell, Perkins, we don't need none o' yer lip. We been savin' yer ass so's you could get away. But ya gotta admit, it was perfect the way the woman went fer a walk with the kid so's we didn't have to storm the house."

Perkin's spit tobacco on the ground. "Yeah, it worked out good. Ya wanna spend the night here or move on?"

The same outlaw answered. "It's best if we keep movin'. Them cowboys is mad as hornets."

The other outlaw asked, "So how's the mother and babe?"

Perkins said, "Hell if I know. I guess they're okay. I ain't heard no cryin'."

June started to stir and fuss as the three men walked into the room.

Perkins dropped his saddlebags on the floor next to the door and the sound startled June. Another cowboy knelt in front of Arizona. "Ma'am, we don't mean ya no harm. We're jus' deliverin' ya to a man who paid fer our services." He bent his head lower to look at Arizona's face covered by her bonnet. She met his gaze straight on. He blinked, blinked again, and then jumped to his feet, shouting, "This ain't the mother!" His loud voice started June screaming and kicking.

Perkins and the other cowboy rushed to the table. Perkins said, "What! Course it is. I saw her last night wearin' that same dress when we was spyin' out the hoedown."

"It ain't her. Take her bonnet off!"

When a hand reached for the ribbons of her bonnet, Arizona insisted, "I'll do it." She pulled the bow apart and one of the men jerked her bonnet from her head. June's screaming intensified.

The third cowboy said, "Hell in a hand basket. Bubba's right."

Perkins put his face in front of hers. "Sheeit!" He stalked across the room and then jerked back around, saying defensively, "I tried to tell ya'll my eyesight's gettin' weak. But I know that's the same dress we saw her in last night and she's the same height. AND SHE WAS CARRYIN' THE KID THIS MORNIN'!" he shouted.

Bubba said to Arizona, "Can you shut that babe up!"

Arizona said above June's screams, "How do you propose I do that? She's hungry and I'm not her mother."

Bubba's eyes rounded and Perkins said, "We gotta get that kid to her destination safe and sound or we're dead men."

The other cowboy agreed. "Yeah, else old man Logan's gonna draw and quarter us."

"Shut up and let me think," said Bubba. He looked at Arizona. "Do you think she can eat jerky?"

Arizona frowned. "Of course not. She needs milk."

Perkins said, "Well, that settles it. Bubba, you gotta go find a milk cow."

Bubba whined, "Why can't Sly?" June let out a piercing wail and Perkins said, "Bubba git yer ass outta here and find some milk for the kid!"

Bubba rubbed his forehead like he had a headache and mumbled, "Why do I always git the crap jobs?"

Chapter 18: Mexican Territory

Arizona sat on the floor where she'd slept. She rocked June and prayed she'd sleep a little longer. Morning light peeked through the one tiny window beside the door and cast shadows across the floor. All night Arizona had tried to keep water down the child by dampening a strip of cloth ripped from her petticoat. June would suck hungrily and then scream when it wasn't milk. The child had finally fallen into an exhausted sleep.

Sitting at the table, Perkins and Sly were brought to attention by a shrill whistle.

"He's back," said Sly, and rushed to open the door.

A few minutes later, Bubba's bulky form filled the doorway and he entered carrying two canteens. Plopping on one of the chairs, he set the canteens on the tabletop and related his story of finding a squatter's cabin, pounding on the door in the dead of night, and thinkin' he'd probably get shot. After fabricating and calling out a story about traveling with his family to a new homestead and his milk cow dyin', with three small children to feed, the door had cracked open. Pointing a rifle at Bubba's chest, a man had asked, "Where's yer fam'ly?"

Bubba said he made up a story about his wife bein' too sick to travel and the children stayin' to care for her. He said with a smirk, "I must'a been convincin' 'cause the wife told one of her boys to go in the cellar and bring up the milk can. They even give me some cheese and bread."

Perkins looked at Arizona and winced when the baby let out a wail. "You think the kid can drink from a canteen?"

Before she could answer, Bubba said proudly, "I got one of them nipples for feedin' babes." He reached into his pocket for it. "I told 'em my wife was too sick to feed the youngest."

Perkins grinned. "You're right smart, Bubba."

Bubba returned his grin. "Hell, by the time I left, them folks was practically beggin' me to bring my fam'ly to come live with 'em."

Sly, said, "I'm right proud o' ya, Bubba."

Bubba stepped in front of Arizona and set a canteen and the nipple on the ground. "Feed the babe afore I slap it silly jus' to shut it up. I ain't slept all night lookin' fer milk."

With courage, Arizona lifted her head and gave him a direct stare. "Bring me some water so I can wash the nipple."

He glared back, but called above June's crying. "Bring a canteen of water, Sly."

After cleaning the nipple and fastening it to the canteen with a piece of leather, Arizona was able to get some nourishment down the baby. For the time being, June quieted. They were soon put back on the horse with Perkins.

* * *

Trent followed the posse's trail and caught up with them before dark. Now tired and disheartened everyone sat around the fire barely making conversation. He was so mad he pounded his fist on the ground. Tim was near death, Daisy was beside herself, Rush had been shot at, June and Arizona were kidnapped, and he felt as helpless as a newborn fawn. He hadn't felt so bad since Katy's death.

The fact that Tim and his sweet family could be torn apart ate at his gut. In a way, Trent had been living vicariously through Tim and Daisy. They were the family he'd wanted to have with Katy.

Lying back and planting his head on his saddle, he watched the fire. His thoughts turned to Arizona. She was a brave woman and he knew she'd protect June with her life. He just needed to figure out where the hell they were being taken. So far, the tracks led south. The way he figured it, they were probably headed for Mexico. If they made it past the Rio Grande, finding them would become more difficult. He'd been to Mexico a handful of times, usually to buy cattle or horses, and he knew a few ranchers. If the kidnappers got that far, he'd contact those ranchers to get the word out about a missing woman and babe.

Before daylight, the posse was up and sipping coffee. As soon as the sun tipped the horizon, they headed out. Mid morning Trent rode up beside Rush. Cutting to the chase, he said, "They're smart. Two horses have been leading us in circles to keep us off a third one's trail—even covering his tracks at times. But they're no match for Grady. He's an expert tracker and knows this country bettr'n we do."

At noon they reached a canyon strewn with rocks and boulders and lost the trail. It took Grady over an hour to find it again. By late afternoon, their travel had slowed to a snail's pace and Trent was fuming.

Rush paced Trent's horse with his own. "Brother, you need to keep your wits about you. If there's one thing I learned in my bounty hunting days, it's that anger gets a man killed, but patience gets the outlaw arrested or killed."

Trent lifted his hat and combed his fingers through sweat drenched hair before settling it back on his head. "You're right. I'm just so mad I want to break their necks. How could anyone kidnap a young woman carrying a babe?"

"Money, brother. I'll just bet someone's paying a hefty price for the kidnapping. Either it's the grandfather like Tim said, or outlaws that sell women and babes. But you need to channel your anger. I have no doubt we'll find them and then you can do whatever you want, but until then, you've got to keep it together." They rode on for a few minutes and then Rush continued, "Usually, I'd advocate for outlaws being brought to justice, but I don't cotton to men stealing women and babies." His meaning was clear as he spurred his horse forward to speak with Grady.

The posse rounded an outcropping of boulders and it was Grady who spotted a crack leading inside the massive formations. By evening they came upon a rustic cabin that had been vacated within the day. Hope soared when Trent found a scrap of Arizona's lavender dress stuffed into a crack in the floor. The woman was smart.

* * *

For hours Arizona's abductors traveled farther into the canyon until they came to a fork. Staying to the left, it wasn't long until they exited the gorge and traveled amongst a scattering of trees that became thicker the farther they journeyed. By evening they reached a creek and camped.

Arizona finished feeding June and said to Perkins, "The milk will be getting blinky soon. We need fresh."

He said a few choice words and looked at Bubba. Bubba said, "It's Sly's turn."

Sly whined, "Why's it my turn? Why can't Perkins go?"

Perkins responded, "Jus' 'cause it's yer turn."

Sly sighed and asked Bubba, "Tell me agin what you said to get the milk."

Before Sly left, Perkins said, "We're gonna come to the Nueces agin in the mornin'. We'll follow the river a few miles using the same route we did gettin' here and then cross over. Then it's straight south to the Rio Grande."

"Okay. I'll find you."

"And you better make it quick so's we don't have to hear that kid screamin' all the way to Mexico."

Arizona held June against her heart. The child was already showing signs of weakness. She whispered, "Baby girl, we're going to be rescued soon. I know Trent will find us."

For the next five days, they traveled from dawn until dusk and Arizona did her best to get June to drink the milk they periodically scrounged up. The baby grew weaker until she no longer screamed; only whimpered when she was hungry. Arizona tried mashing cheese and bread with the milk and that seemed to satisfy the child for longer periods of time.

When they reached the Rio Grande, she told the men for the hundredth time, "We've got to find someone to nurse this child or she won't live much longer."

Perkins finally said, "Okay, I believe ya. I got a woman in mind." He turned to Sly and Bubba. "We'll head to Poncho's place out past Nuevo Laredo. I'll send a wire to old man Logan and tell him he can pick the babe up there. I want to be rid of this kid afore somethin' happens to her.

Sly eyed Arizona. "What about her?"

Perkins shrugged. "She's the old man's problem, not ours."

A day later, after crossing the Rio Grande at a low spot and traversing rocky terrain, they came to the outskirts of a dusty town. The men dismounted and left her and June on Perkins' horse. She heard them talking softly.

"…Poncho's wife…take about half a day…"

"The old man's gonna kill us…babe dies. Maybe we should cut our losses and…"

"Are you crazy, Slim. If we…we're dead fer sure. Least ways…kid has a chance with Poncho's wife."

Arizona was shifted to Sly's horse and Perkins took off for town, she supposed, to send the wire.

Skirting the town, Sly and Bubba headed into vacant territory of rocks, dust, scrub brush, and heat. Since being kidnapped, Arizona had done everything in her power to remain vigilant over June, but days of endless travel, poor food, little water, and sleepless nights had taken a toll on her health. Lifting her eyes heavenward, she prayed for strength and then whispered to June, "Just a little farther, sweetheart."

During the hottest part of the day, they finally arrived at their destination—a small sod home with a pitiful looking corral. Inside the corral a few mules lazily watched their approach. For all the shabbiness of the homestead, the animals looked well cared for. Even the garden planted between the house and the corral was thriving. The barn was another soddy where a horse and milk cow could be seen inside. Chickens scattered in the wake of the new arrivals.

A rifle slipped through the opening of a window beside the door and then was pulled back inside. The door opened and a short, stocky, Mexican man chewing on the end of a cigar, sauntered outside. He grinned and said with a heavy accent, "Welcome, mis amigos. It has been many months since we meet. What trouble has found you now?" He moved his gaze to Arizona and the babe.

Sly and Bubba dismounted and approached the Mexican. Beyond the doorway, Arizona could see a woman holding a squirming baby about June's age.

The men shook hands and Bubba said, "We got hired to deliver this kid and her ma to Rio Bravo in Texas, but the woman ain't the babe's kin. We've had a helluva time keepin' the kid fed. We need a woman to suckle her." He pushed his hat back. "We'll pay ya if'n yer woman can feed her."

Poncho eyed Arizona again and puffed on his cigar. He turned toward the soddy and shouted, "Maria, ven!"

Arizona watched Maria place her baby in a cradle before venturing outside to stand beside her husband. He spoke in Spanish and pointed toward Arizona and June. Arizona met the woman's gaze and held it. In Maria's eyes she saw kindness.

Sly helped Arizona from his horse and while she got her land legs, Maria approached. Arizona lifted the blanket for her to see June. She didn't know if Maria could understand English, but she said with a sob, "She's so weak. I've been giving her cow's milk, but it doesn't sit well with her."

Maria reached for June and spoke soothing words in Spanish. Whether she was talking to her or June, Arizona was unsure. She swallowed back tears and again saw kindness in the woman's eyes. She released her grip on the child. Maria hummed softly as she walked back to the soddy with June. Arizona followed her inside and barely glanced around the small home. Maria sat in a rocker beside a woven straw bed and opened her bodice. June was so weak she barely whimpered and tears gushed down Arizona's cheeks. Could she have done more to save this baby?

After several attempts, June rallied and latched onto Maria's breast. Arizona wiped a hand across her eyes and relief flooded her when the child suckled. Maria made a waving motion toward the bed and

Arizona collapsed onto it. Her legs felt so weak she most certainly would have soon fallen.

When Maria began singing softly, Arizona closed her eyes. Listening to Maria's lovely voice was the last thing she remembered before losing consciousness.

Chapter 19: Brand

At a farm not far from the Rio Grande on the Texas side, Trent sat atop his horse and stared down at a farmer pointing a rifle at him. Rush and the other posse members steadied their horses behind him. They must have been a formidable looking group because the man with the rifle didn't waver and his wife, peeking from a window, looked terrified.

Trent said, "We're a posse looking for a kidnapped white woman and babe."

Something sparked in the man's eyes, but he gruffly replied, "Ain't seen no woman with a babe."

Trent narrowed his eyes. "The babe's in grave danger because the woman's not her mother and can't feed her."

The farmer's eyes widened. Before he could respond, the door opened and the woman who had been peeking through the window stepped out. Her husband ordered without turning around. "Git back in the house! I can take care of this."

Disregarding his command, she stepped beside her husband. "There was a man come to our door a few nights back and said he needed milk 'cause his cow died. He said his wife was sick and couldn't nurse their babe. We took pity on him and filled his canteens."

Trent asked, "How many nights ago?"

Her husband lowered his rifle and responded, "'Bout three, I reckon."

"Did you see the woman or babe?"

This time the wife said, "No, sir."

"Did the man give any clue as to where he was headed?"

"No, sorry."

Trent lifted his hat in frustration and ran a hand through his hair. "Which way did he go when he left?"

"He headed south," said the farmer.

Trent nodded. "Thank you kindly. At least we know they passed this way."

He started to turn his horse around when the man spoke again. "Ah, don't know if this helps, but I recognized the brand on the man's horse. It's a ranch on the Mexican side although I can't remember the name."

Hope sprang up in Trent.

Rush urged his horse forward. "Can you draw the brand for us?"

"Yes, sir."

Both Trent and Rush dismounted and followed the man to his porch and waited while he went inside. Shortly, he returned with a paper on which he'd drawn the brand.

Trent said, "That mark's not familiar to me." He glanced at Rush who shook his head.

Rush said, "We'll show it to the men."

Trent sounded optimistic, "There are a lot of ranchos on the Mexican side, but at least we got a lead. Since losing the trail, I'll take anything I can get."

The brothers thanked the farmer and his wife, hurried back to their mounts, and galloped toward Mexico.

* * *

Arizona woke with a start. Her heart pounded; something was amiss. She reoriented herself—she had given the care of June over to a Mexican woman. Sunlight filtered through gunny-sack curtains from a window above the bed.

Where's June?

She heard singing. It was the voice of the woman named Maria. Jumping off the bed she scanned the dim interior of the sod home. The woman had moved her rocker to sit beside a fireless hearth. In her lap were two babies, June and the child Arizona had seen earlier. Both children slept peacefully.

Relief almost brought Arizona to her knees. The woman smiled. In accented English, she said, "Baby good."

Arizona rushed to kneel beside the rocker. Softly, she touched June's cheek. "Gracious, Señora Maria."

Maria smiled and then lifted June toward Arizona.

Arizona accepted the baby and sat in one of two chairs next to the only table. Not knowing if Maria would understand her question, she asked, "What is your baby's name?"

"Catalina Maria Elena Arroyo Padilla."

"That's beautiful. What should I call her?"

Maria laughed. "She is Princesa." After a long, but comfortable silence, Maria said, "I make food for you." She rose and laid her baby in a cradle at the foot of her bed.

Arizona was so hungry she didn't argue. Within a few minutes, Maria had set a plate of frijoles and corn tortillas in front of her. Maria reached to hold June. "You eat."

With a grateful smile, Arizona handed June over and ate the most flavorful food she'd ever tasted. While she satisfied her hunger, Maria sat across from her and they conversed in broken Spanish and broken English.

Arizona learned that Maria and her husband worked a small ranch and Princesa was there only child. They had lost twin boys to fever three years previous. Arizona said, "I'm so sorry."

Maria fingered a tear. "Now we have new baby."

Arizona smiled. The fact that they were conversing as if they were neighbors enjoying a friendly afternoon was not lost on Arizona. She needed information. Casually, she said, "I was kidnapped by the men who brought me here."

Maria glanced away.

Arizona forged on. "I don't know their intentions, but they weren't happy when they discovered I wasn't June's mother. I fear for the child if they kill me."

Maria jerked her eyes to Arizona's.

The door opened and Poncho entered with Perkins.

Chapter 20: Tracking Clues

Trent and his posse were met with curious glances when they rode into Nuevo Laredo. Before entering town, they had decided to pretend they were ranchers looking to buy strong mounts. They located the saloon and dismounted. Entering the dim interior, Trent led the way past a half dozen card tables. A few players watched their progress toward the bar, but most were too engrossed in their cards to give them more than passing attention.

Trent, Rush, Tad, Slim, Grady, and the five hands with them, waited for the bartender to pour a drink for another customer at the end of the bar. With a bored expression, the short Mexican glanced their way. "What you drink?" he asked.

Trent said, "Bottle of Tequila, mi amigo."

Rush interjected, "Shot glasses for everyone." He waved toward his men.

The bartender lifted a bottle of tequila from a shelf mounted below a risqué picture and clunked it in front of Trent. He then reached under the bar and grabbed glasses, setting one in front of each cowboy.

The men made small talk for several minutes before Rush slipped a paper from his pocket and said to the bartender. "We're lookin' to buy horses for our ranch in Texas. We met up with a fella who said some of the best mounts can be bought from the ranch with this brand. He couldn't remember the name, though. Sure hope you can point us in the right direction." He slid the paper across the counter toward the bartender. The man glanced at the drawing, pulled on his handlebar mustache and said in broken English, "I make drinks. No answer questions."

Rush didn't respond. He pulled the paper back in front of him and leisurely poured another shot of whiskey.

A tall Mexican wearing dusty chaps and wicked looking spurs, stepped next to Trent. He stared past Trent at Rush. "For a drink. I might have the information you want."

Rush pushed the drawing toward him.

The Mexican looked down. Without lifting the paper, he said, "That's Rancho de Paraiso. It's about twenty miles south."

"Much obliged for the information, sir." Rush slipped the paper back in his pocket. "Order your drink."

The man smiled and shifted his gaze to the bartender. "I'll have the same as them."

The bartender lifted a shot glass to the counter, but the man said, "Not a shot…a bottle."

The bartender glanced at Rush who nodded his agreement.

For the next hour, Trent and Rush talked small-talk with the Mexican and anyone else who turned friendly. A busty woman sidled up beside them and they continued the game, flirting with her. For all intents and purposes, no one had reason to suspect they were other than who they purported to be. By the time they left the bar, even the bartender was laughing with them. Finally, they called friendly goodbyes and headed out of town.

After they reached the outskirts, Trent lifted a hand to soothe the headache that racked his temple. Rush trotted beside him and rubbed his own temple. "I'm with you, brother. That whole scene made my head pound."

"Damn tequila didn't help."

By late afternoon they reached the elaborate entrance to Rancho de Paraiso. The beautiful hacienda appeared cool and inviting. Trent glanced at Rush, "I can understand why they named it Paradise Ranch." He gave instructions to his posse to wait at the gate while he and Rush inquired for information. From the large numbers of corralled horses and the ones roaming the range beyond the outbuildings, the operation was evidently a successful one. Several Mexicans turned from their duties to give them passing interest as they approached, but that was all they did. Eventually, a tall sun-bronzed Mexican whose golden hair made him stand out from the others exited one of three barns and walked toward them. As he walked, he removed his gloves, slapped them against his thigh, and then dusted his chaps. He was lean, muscular, and gave the impression of one used to wielding authority.

Rush said, "I sure as hell wouldn't want to tangle with him."

"You got that right."

Trent and Rush dismounted and walked their horses forward. Trent's gut feeling was that honesty would be best when he saw the man's clear blue eyes and friendly smile.

The handsome Mexican spoke in perfect English. "Hello, my fellow Americans."

That piqued Trent's interest. "Are we that obvious?"

The man shrugged and held out his hand. "My name is Marcus Rodriguez. Welcome to my father's ranch, Rancho de Paraiso. My father is visiting relatives in Mexico City, so I am in charge. Please call me Marcus."

Trent shook his hand. "Trent Garrett." He motioned to Rush. "My brother, Rush."

Marcus asked, "Are you the owners of Big G Ranch?"

Surprised again, Trent said, "We are. Didn't know anyone this far out would have heard of us."

Marcus replied, "I occasionally travel to the states to visit my American family. Your ranch may be small compared to others, but it is well spoken of. What can I do for you? Are you looking to buy horses or cattle?"

Trent scuffed his boot in the dirt, studied it, and then lifted his head. Unflinching, he stared into Marcus' eyes. "A woman and babe were kidnapped from our ranch. I've got a posse waiting outside your entrance. We lost the trail a few days back and are following clues."

Marcus didn't remove his gaze from Trent's. "And those clues brought you here?"

"They did. Seems one of the kidnappers was riding a horse with your brand."

"We sometimes sell horses with our brand so that doesn't mean any of our men are involved."

"I understand that. But right now, you're the only lead we've got and we fear for the lives of the woman and babe."

"I'll do everything I can to help. Tell me what you know. Can you describe this horse?"

Trent nodded at Rush to continue. While Rush explained the circumstances of finding out about the horse from the homesteaders and gave the description, Trent studied Marcus. The man's eyes remained steady. Trent was almost positive he could be trusted.

Marcus said, "That description fits many of our horses. What of the man, can you describe him?"

Rush said, "This is what the farmer told us." He then proceeded to describe the kidnapper. After that, he related the kidnapping of Arizona and June, the wounding of the baby's father, his and Trent's own narrow escape, and then tracking the outlaws. He revealed that Arizona was not the child's mother and that the kidnappers had gone in search of milk for the babe.

Marcus listened intently.

Rush said, "That's all we have to go on."

Marcus responded, "We had a ranch hand working here that perhaps meets your description. He also bought a horse like the one you described. His name is George Perkinson, but everyone calls him Perkins. He quit about a month ago and I haven't seen him since. I'll ask my men if they know his whereabouts." He paused. "And I'll be discreet. I won't let anyone know why I'm asking."

Trent stuck out his hand. "That's more than fair. Thank you."

Rush said, "We noticed a nice stand of trees about a quarter mile back beside a stream. If it's on your property would you mind if we camped there. We can check with you in the morning to see what you've found out."

"Yes, I know the place. It's on our land and, of course, you may camp there."

After shaking hands with Marcus, Trent and Rush mounted their steeds and headed back toward their men. Rush said, "I hope to hell he learns something useful."

A vision of Arizona's adorable expression when she was giving him holy hell popped into Trent's mind. His gut knotted. He *had* to find her.

Chapter 21: Maria

Arizona lay on a blanket on the floor with June cradled against her. Over the past three days the baby had improved until she was once again cooing and smiling. Although not completely recovered, with continued regular feedings she soon would be.

Their kidnappers had taken up residence in the pitiful looking barn. Often Arizona would see Maria and her husband whispering or exchanging glances. She didn't know whether they were privy to her and June's fate. Whenever the opportunity arose, she begged Maria for help in escaping Perkins and his men. Maria always found distractions to remove herself from Arizona's presence.

On her fourth day at Poncho and Maria's rancho, another man showed up mid morning. He was probably over fifty, but less than sixty years of age. He had the look of one accustomed to wealth and having his orders obeyed. When he arrived, Arizona was sitting outside the soddy and holding June. The new arrival rode to within a few feet of Arizona and dismounted.

Perkins rushed from the barn, pulling up his suspenders, while Bubba and Sly waited in the entrance, shifting their stance from one foot to the other and looking nervous.

Perkins, with his hair awry, said tensely, "Mr. Logan, I see you got our wire. We-we got yer goods." He motioned toward Arizona and June.

The man looked at Perkins with such disgust, he stepped backward.

Mr. Logan said, "Apparently, you only retrieved half of my *goods*. This isn't the child's mother. I see why you summoned me from Rio Bravo. Where's Daisy?"

"Uh-well, I need to talk to you about that, sir. Seems, well, this woman was walkin' with the child and wearin' the same clothes the mother had been wearin' and, well, there was a mix-up. By the time we discovered it we was on the road and it was too late to turn back and, well..." His voice faltered.

Mr. Logan looked past Perkins to Bubba and Sly and they visibly shrank backward. The man inhaled deeply, looked at Arizona and demanded, "Who are you?"

Rather than antagonize him, she said politely, "My name is Arizona Cayson."

He looked from Arizona to Maria standing in the doorway holding her own babe. Understanding crossed his features. He said, "So you're feeding the child?"

Maria replied, "Si, señor."

Maria's husband rounded the corner of the soddy leading a horse. He stopped and warily appraised the stranger.

Mr. Logan directed his attention toward Poncho. "Are you the head of this house?"

"Si, señor."

"I'd like to speak privately with you." The glance the new arrival cast toward Arizona sent shivers down her spine.

Throughout the day, Arizona was frustrated by being relegated to the inside of the house with June. The two windows in the soddy were so dirty she could barely see outdoors. Maria remained outside most of the time with Princesa. At noon, she returned and Arizona helped her prepare a meal. She refused to answer Arizona's questions or even meet her gaze. Poncho and Mr. Logan entered the house when Maria called them inside. The men spoke little and Arizona's gut instinct told her that her situation had turned dire with this man's arrival. Throughout her capture, she had gleaned from listening to Perkins and his men that Mr. Logan was June's grandfather. When she turned to flip a tortilla, she caught Maria's eye and soundlessly beseeched her for help. Maria quickly averted her gaze.

As soon as Mr. Logan finished his meal he motioned toward Poncho and then left the soddy without a word. Poncho glanced at his wife and then followed Mr. Logan outside.

Arizona tried to speak with Maria but she whispered fiercely, "No talk!"

* * *

For two days, the posse camped on Rancho de Paraiso land while Marcus Hernandez questioned his ranch hands. Because some of the men were on the range moving cattle, he had ridden out to personally speak with them. He returned without helpful information.

Trent slapped his hat against his thigh in frustration. "Any idea as to where we should go next?

We're not leaving Mexico until we find our woman and babe."

Marcus rubbed his jaw. "I suggest you return to Nuevo Laredo and make inquires. I'll send two of my men with you. My name will add respect."

Rush said, "Thanks, Marcus. We'll take all the help we can get."

The brothers started to turn away, but Trent hesitated. "Do you have any squatters on your land?"

Marcus nodded. "We do. The closest is about fifteen miles due east. Then there's a family south about thirty miles and another southeast maybe fifty miles. Why?"

Trent repositioned his hat and straightened the brim. "Don't take this the wrong way, but from experience I've learned that squatters are sometimes privy to more information than the landowner. If it's all right with you, I'd like to ride to the closest one and ask questions. If I leave at daybreak, I'll be back by late afternoon."

Marcus said, "No offense taken. You're welcome on my land."

Rush said, "I'm coming with you."

* * *

Lying on a pallet on the floor with June, Arizona envisioned every scenario she could for escape. Her situation appeared hopeless but she refused to believe there was no way out. Her head ached from all the stress.

Shifting sounds behind Poncho and Maria's curtain caught her attention. Her eyes were accustomed to the darkness and she saw Maria step beyond the drape, followed by Poncho. Maria walked over and knelt beside her.

Arizona whispered, "I'm awake."

Maria rasped, "We hurry!" Her baby had been securely wrapped against her body.

Alert to any escape opportunity, Arizona always slept in her dress. Even though the women had washed it, it barely resembled the once beautiful gown, not that that mattered any more. Hastily she stood and accepted the strip of cloth Maria held out to her. Quickly and efficiently, the women secured June to her body. The baby whimpered, but did not come fully awake. Arizona asked, "Where are we going?"

Maria did not answer.

In the shadows, Arizona could see Poncho near the hearth. He removed an old rug and then lifted some boards. Maria helped Arizona into her shoes before pulling her toward Poncho. His face was in shadow, but his body language spoke volumes. He reached a hand around his wife's neck and pulled her toward him. Arizona could hear them kiss and whisper tender words. Maria broke away and Poncho helped her into the hole that had been revealed under the boards. Arizona felt his hand on her arm. He urged her forward. "Vaya con Dios," were his final words as he assisted her into a space about four feet deep. She heard Maria say, "Come."

With her heart in her throat, Arizona bent forward and entered a tunnel, listening for the sounds of Maria in front of her. Once, when June started to cry, she feared the worst. They would be discovered and June ripped from her arms. Tears sprang to her eyes. She just *had* to save this baby.

Sounds of Maria's humming softly floated back to them and June quieted. The black void seemed endless. For at least thirty minutes they slowly moved forward. Arizona's back hurt from being bent over and her legs cramped. She stumbled a few times.

Fresh air suddenly replaced the dank and dusty smell and Arizona breathed deeply. The tunnel ended and she stepped inside a large, shadowed room. An opening revealed twinkling stars and she could see the moon. They were inside a cave.

Maria said, "Hurry this way."

Arizona disregarded the aches of her body and hastened forward. At the cave's mouth, Maria paused and pointed. "There is home."

Across the desert landscape the soddy and barn were barely visible. The passage had brought them a long ways to a place of higher elevation scattered with large boulders and palo verde trees amongst scrub brush.

Maria darted out of the cave. June whimpered and Arizona patted her back, praying the child wouldn't cry.

Suddenly, Maria stopped.

Arizona heard a sound and froze. Tilting her head to see beyond Maria, she saw something large—a horse. Already the Mexican woman had her foot in the stirrup, hoisting herself up. She reached toward Arizona and soon both women and their babies hastened away from danger. As the horse clomped forward under Maria's expert guidance, Arizona felt a surge of hope.

Chapter 22: Brave Women

Throughout their escape, Maria kept the horse at a slow but steady pace. The long ride gave Arizona time to ask questions of the woman who had saved her and June. The first question was, "Did you dig that tunnel?"

Maria laughed softly, "No, we find when looking for place to build la casa. Poncho say someday maybe we need."

"Where are we going?"

"To Rancho de Paraiso. It is big rancho. Have good people to help."

Finally, Arizona asked the question that had been burning in her mind. "They were going to kill me, weren't they?"

Maria hesitated, and then answered, "Yes. Kill you then take me with them. They offer Poncho much money and he—how you say—pretend good idea. But he know we have to leave."

"Why didn't he come with us?"

Arizona could hear distress in Maria's voice. "He keep bad men away long as he can."

Tears sprang to Arizona's eyes. "How can I ever repay this kindness?"

"It is not kindness. It is—how you say—duty. Poncho and me have to stop bad men."

Toward dawn, the babies woke and while Arizona tried to keep June quiet by placing her finger in the child's mouth to suckle, Maria nursed Princesa. As soon as she was satisfied, the women traded babies so June could be nursed.

The sun rose and so did fear in Arizona's heart. They now traveled flat desert. Maria stopped long enough for them the stretch their legs, drink water from a canteen, and eat jerky stowed in the saddlebag.

Arizona gazed at June's smiling face and whispered, "I'll give my life for you if it comes to that." She looked up to see Maria watching her.

They continued onward and the terrain changed again into boulders and scrawny trees. Unexpectedly, a rattler crossed their path and their horse danced sideways before rearing upright and almost toppling Arizona to the ground. Maria, being an excellent horsewoman, made short work of calming the beast.

Arizona knew Maria was pushing their horse as fast as safely possible and when she asked how much farther, Maria pointed. "Over that hill we see rancho far away."

Air whooshed from Arizona's lungs that freedom was so close. Throughout her captivity she had often thought of Trent and how he was wasting his life pining over a dead woman. She had decided that if she escaped this nightmare, she would give him a lecture about letting go of the past and living in the present.

As she did periodically, Arizona glanced behind them to discover her worst fear. Men on horses were fast approaching. She shouted to Maria, "They've found us!"

Maria yelled something in Spanish, and then, "Hold on!" She spurred their steed. The horse broke into a gallop, but Arizona knew outrunning the men was impossible. She and Maria had already discussed what they would do if pursued. The change in atmosphere from quiet speculation to a death run, started the babies screaming.

While Maria headed for rocky outcroppings on the hill, Arizona was already untying June from her wrapping. Behind a large boulder Maria jerked their horse to a halt and the women dismounted. Arizona handed June to Maria and swiftly they wrapped the baby next to Princesa. The women worked in silence, knowing the inevitable. When June was secured to Maria, Arizona slid the shotgun out of its scabbard. Summoning her courage, she said, "Maria, Go with God. Save the babies."

Tears dripped down Maria's cheeks but she wasted no time in mounting her steed. Arizona slapped the rump of the horse. She didn't even watch them ride away. Quickly, she climbed a boulder and peeked over it. In the distance dust stirred and she could see the outline of three horses. Positioning herself for the best angle, she readied her shotgun. And waited.

* * *

Since leaving Rancho de Paraiso, Trent had second guessed his decision to travel fifteen miles to ask questions of a squatter family. Was he wasting precious time?

Rush seemed to read his mind. "Riding out here was as good a choice as any."

"I certainly hope so."

Trent heard something. "Did you hear that?"

They halted their horses and listened. Rush replied, "I don't hear anything."

Trent shook his head. "God, I'm losing it. I could have sworn I heard a baby crying."

Rush gave him a surprised look—and then they both heard it. Rush gasped, "That *is* a baby's cry!"

Immediately the men kicked their horses into gallops. Trent pointed. "Look, over there."

In the distance a single rider was running a horse. Trent and Rush turned their mounts in that direction and rode hard. Shortly, Rush yelled, "It's a woman."

The mystery rider slowed and so did they. At twenty feet out, amidst a baby's wail, Trent called, "Do you need help? We're looking for a woman and a babe that were kidnapped on the U.S. side."

The Mexican woman replied, "I have baby June."

Trent and Rush galloped forward and Trent's heart dove to the ground. Where was Arizona?

When they came closer, the men could see two babies wrapped against the woman.

She said, "Arizona hide in rocks." She turned in her saddle and pointed. "She have shotgun. Banditos coming."

The sound of gunfire cracked the air.

Rush said, "Do you know where Rancho de Paraiso is?"

"Yes, we go there."

"Good. Tell Marcus Hernandez to send help."

Without waiting for an answer, Trent galloped in the direction of gunshots. Rush caught up with him. Return fire could be heard beyond the hill. At the base, both men scrambled off their horses and secured the reins to scrub brush. With shotguns in hand, they rushed toward the sound of Arizona's gunfire.

Trent shouted, "Arizona, its Trent and Rush! Don't shoot us!"

He peeked around a boulder and her widened eyes met his. She then did something that forever captured his heart—she smiled. He said, "We're here, darlin'."

Gunfire from the outlaws interrupted the moment. Rush said, "I'm going back for my horse. If you two can keep the outlaws entertained, I'll circle behind them, forcing them into the open."

Trent said, "Rush, I'll go. You have a family and I'd never forgive myself if something happened to you."

Before Rush could argue, Trent memorized Arizona's sweet face with a glance and then backtracked down the hill. He heard her call, "There are three of them."

Mounting his steed, the intelligent horse skirted the hill following his every command, and then galloped further into the desert. Finally, he turned his horse back toward the hill. Pausing beside a palo verde tree, the only cover close enough to shoot from, he dismounted and lay in the sand, waiting. Shots rang out again and just as he had hoped, one of the kidnappers raised his head above his rock hideout to take aim.

Trent fired. POP! The outlaw fell forward. One down, but the others were now aware of him; the scrawny tree wasn't much cover. He started to mount his horse, but another shot rang out and white hot pain seared Trent's upper right chest.

"Damn!" he shouted.

Sudden fire from the hill hit an outlaw and he yelled in agony before slumping over the top of a rock. The other cowboy moved to pull his screaming comrade to safety. Ignoring his own pain, Trent aimed, sighted, and pressed the trigger. The man went down.

Trent leaned against the tree and whipped his bandana from his pocket, pressing it to his wound. He was losing a lot of blood. Not sure if the kidnappers were dead, and praying no one could take aim, he whistled for his horse who had wandered several feet away. Venus trotted back to him. Holding himself against the side of his animal for protection, he slapped her rump to urge her into a run. After they had gone a safe distance, he hauled himself atop his horse and started back toward Arizona and Rush. They met him halfway with Arizona riding behind Rush.

He must have looked bad because Arizona lifted her hand to her mouth and sobbed. He smiled. "Hell, Arizona, you just fought off banditos without so much as a tear. Don't waste cryin' on me."

Rush said, "Brother, if you die, I'll never forgive you. We got a long ride."

Trent ground his jaw against the pain. "I can make it."

Chapter 23: Return to Sanity

For Trent, the return to Rancho de Paraiso seemed an eternity. Rush and Arizona had removed his shirt and torn it into strips, wrapping his upper chest tightly. Arizona now rode behind him holding her hand over the wound. The bleeding had stopped, but the pain had not.

Finally, they were met by Marcus and his men and the posse from Big G. Trent and Arizona were transferred to fresh horses while Marcus and two of his hands, as well as Arizona's brothers and Grady, accompanied them back to the ranch. The other Big G and Rancho de Paraiso men continued onward to the place where the outlaws had been shot and also to Maria's soddy to check on Poncho's fate.

By the time Trent entered the ornate entrance to the rancho, he was drifting in and out of consciousness. He had so much he wanted to say to Arizona, but he couldn't stay focused. Sometimes he was in the present, and sometimes he was again by Katy's bedside just before she died. The baby was already dead, but she wouldn't let loose of her.

Trent yelled in emotional and physical agony. In a black tunnel he heard a voice say, "Hurry, men, get him to the bed." He fought the darkness and felt his hands and feet being tied down. He struggled until he heard a soft voice speaking in his ear. "Please Trent, let us help you."

"Arizona?" he rasped.

More whispered words. "I'm right here beside you."

Her presence eased his pain and the darkness didn't frighten him as much. In fact, there was a faraway light that kept getting brighter. He stilled and waited for it. The light pulsed and he could see rays emanating from its core, reaching toward him—enfolding him in peace.

"Katy?"

"Hello, my love."

He started to cry. "I've missed you so much."

"I'm always with you."

"Can I stay here with you?"

"If you wish. But do you really want to? If you allow yourself to love again, you can have a beautiful life with children you adore."

"Where's our baby?"

"She's with me. And just as I'm always with you, so is she."

"I don't understand."

"Of course you don't. There are mysteries only revealed on this side."

"Rush has come home."

"I know."

"He's forgiven me."

"Of course he has. He's a wonderful man who's found peace with Lilah and their children. I want you to find that same peace."

"If I go with you, will I find it?"

"You will. But do you really want to leave Arizona?"

After a long silence, he responded, "No. She makes me feel again."

"So, see, you have your answer."

"Katy?"

"Yes, my dearest?"

"Thank you."

The light began slowly retreating. Trent watched until it was a soft glow. In his mind, Katy said softly, "Your loved ones are always with you."

* * *

Arizona dipped a cloth in a bowl and wrung the water out. She soothed Trent's forehead. A cot had been moved into the bedroom so she could stay with him. Rush and the man named Marcus, as well as the doctor he'd summoned, had tried to talk her into resting in one of the guest rooms, but she was unwilling to leave. She thanked God that Trent's fever had recently broken. The day before, the doctor had removed the bullet and cauterized the wound. The smell of burning flesh still lingered, making her stomach queasy.

She dipped the cloth again. When her gaze returned to his face, she gasped. His eyes were open and he was watching her with a sane expression.

"Trent. You're back."

A slow smile tilted his lips. Barely above a whisper, he said, "That I am, darlin'."

Arizona swiped sudden tears.

He reached his good arm and touched her hand. "I'm so sorry."

"For what?"

"For being a blind jackass."

Arizona blinked. Was he going delirious again?

He closed his eyes. "I'm so tired. We'll talk later." He drifted into peaceful sleep.

Chapter 24: Decisions

Over the next week, Arizona was amazed by Trent's rapid recovery. Doc Delgado said he'd cheated the Angel of Death. Trent's cryptic response had been, "I met an angel, but it wasn't the Angel of Death."

As for Maria, her wild flight with two babies strapped to her was the talk of the rancho. Marcus said the heroic escape of two women with two babies would become legendary. Arizona had no desire to become a legend. She was just happy the babies were thriving and Poncho had been found alive. None of the men who found him thought he would survive the long ride back to the rancho. However, he not only survived, he revived enough to sit atop a horse and sling curses at the dead kidnappers and Mr. Logan. By the time they reached Rancho de Paraiso, Poncho was fuming and the doc had to give him laudanum to calm him. Later he told everyone that he'd *demanded* God keep him from dying; he wasn't ready to leave his wife and child.

As soon as Trent was stronger, Rush and Arizona sat at his bedside to decide their options in returning home.

Arizona said, "We can pack milk to take with us but it will sour quickly and we'll have to locate other cows, or we could bring a cow with us, but frankly, June doesn't take well to cow's milk. And even if Daisy were brought here, her milk will have dried up long ago."

Rush said, "So Maria needs to accompany us, which means two babies will make the long journey."

Arizona interjected, "And she'd have to leave Poncho because he's in no shape to travel."

Leaning against the headboard of his bed, Trent said, "The other option is to wait until Poncho recovers and ask him to come too."

Rush responded, "Don't forget he has his ranch to run. For the time being, Marcus has sent hands to care for the animals."

Arizona said, "There's another problem."

Trent and Rush waited for her to continue.

"The mastermind behind the kidnapping is still at large. We have no idea what he has in mind."

Trent cursed and Rush ran a hand through his hair. Rush said, "What the hell are we going to do?"

Chapter 25: Fatted Calf

Daisy scooped water into a pitcher and poured it over Tim's back as he took his first bath. The tub that had belonged to Trent and Rush's mother had been moved into their room. He'd grown stronger over the past week and was able to walk and sit for short periods. His emaciated body was now gaining weight, but his attitude, after three weeks of convalescing, alternated between cranky and depressed.

Gently rubbing a cloth over his wound that was pink and tender, Daisy saw him wince. Leaning forward, she kissed his cheek and whispered, "I've not given up hope, and neither should you."

Tim turned sad eyes on her and they stared at each other offering comfort without words.

A loud knock sounded on their door and Pearl shouted. "Daisy! Tim! We got a wire from Rush!"

Disregarding Tim's undressed state, Daisy ran to the door and threw it open. Pearl rushed in, glanced at Tim covering himself with his hands, and said, "Don't bother, son. You ain't got nothin' I ain't seen." She pulled Daisy into a hug. "June's been found and they's all safe and sound."

If Pearl hadn't been hugging Daisy, she would have fallen to the ground. "Oh, my baby, my baby!" she cried. She turned joyous eyes on Tim who had half risen from the tub. He said, "One of you hand me a towel."

Pearl said, "Daisy, you go sit on the bed afore you faint from happiness."

Daisy obeyed and Pearl reached for a towel, tossing it at Tim. "I'm gonna leave the wire here on the table. It don't say more'n that, but I gots a feelin' we'll hear more soon. Right now, I gots to inform ever-body 'bout this happy turn of events."

After Pearl left, Tim approached Daisy with the towel wrapped around his waist and sat beside her. Tears streamed down her face. She laid her head against his good shoulder. Gently, he lowered his head to kiss her temple. "I love you, Daisy."

* * *

Daisy, along with the entire Big G household, was on pins-and-needles waiting for another wire. When a courier from town rode to the ranch three days later, everyone burst into the yard and surrounded his horse before he could dismount. Since the kidnapping, the entire community, even folks from long distances, had brought food and offered assistance for anything needed by the family.

The middle-aged messenger had barely dismounted when a buckboard driven by Arizona's father rolled into the yard.

Pearl took charge. Placing her fingers to her teeth, she whistled shrilly. The sound brought immediate silence. She reached her hand out for the wire. Quickly, she opened it, lifted the page, and silently read.

Then she read aloud.

LEAVING 25 AUG. BRINGING WET NURSE AND TWO BABIES. EXPECTED ARRIVAL 31 AUG. RUSH

When Pearl read the last word, the crowd shouted and started hugging one another. Daisy threw her arms around Tim, forgetting about his wound, until he grunted. She jerked backward, but he darted his hand around her waist and pulled her back against him. She glanced over his shoulder to see Huck Cayson with a big smile cracking his usually stern countenance.

Pearl yelled above the chaos, "This calls for a feast. Tonight we're eating the fatted calf!"

* * *

One day before the anticipated arrival of her baby, Daisy was in the kitchen helping Pearl when Tim rushed in. He pulled her into his arms. "Honey, June's home."

Pearl dropped the spoon into the stew pot and lifted her hands in the air. "Thank ya, Lord, for yer sweet mercies!"

For a moment, Daisy couldn't move. Tears sprang to her eyes when Tim lifted her hand to his mouth and kissed it, his expression revealing his love for her and the baby. Savoring the moment, she reached to smooth his hair. "Our baby's home."

Tim gave her the smile she loved and she clasped his hand. Together they rushed toward the front door. Pearl was right behind them. They ran toward the returning posse. In the forefront sat two women on steeds, a Mexican woman and Arizona. Both women had a babe tied to her body.

Tim, still recovering from his wound, released Daisy's hand. "Honey, you run ahead. I'm right behind you."

Daisy looked up at him. "No, Tim, we'll do this together." Again, he gave her his endearing smile. Hand in hand, they hurried toward their baby.

Trent stepped to assist Arizona from her horse. She tried to untie June from her body but Daisy could see her hands were trembling. The moment was so emotional Daisy started crying. Tim pulled her against his side.

Trent said to Arizona, "Let me untie her." Arizona wiped her eyes and said with a wobbly voice, "I think that would be a good idea."

Trent released June from Arizona's body and lifted the squalling babe. Cradling her to his chest, he turned, kissed the top of her head, and then handed her to Daisy. The baby suddenly stopped crying, blinked several times, and then grinned at her mother.

Daisy made a joyous, but unintelligible sound, and everyone started brushing away tears. She was so engrossed in loving her baby that she wasn't aware of the woman and child beside Arizona until Trent said, "Tim and Daisy, I'd like you to meet Maria Margarita Padilla Hernandez de Arroyo and her daughter, Catalina Maria Elena. She and her husband Poncho saved June and Arizona from the kidnappers."

Through tears, Daisy choked, "I am forever in your debt." She looked at Arizona, "Thank you for your courage."

Tim echoed her gratitude, "We can never repay either of you for what you have done."

Maria shyly smiled and Catalina reached a chubby hand toward June.

June kicked her legs and reached back.

Daisy said, "I think they'll be friends forever."

Arizona smoothed a hand down Catalina's curls. "We call her Princesa."

Pearl stepped from the sidelines. "This calls for a banquet tonight!"

That evening, around another feast prepared by Pearl, there was a recounting of the events of the past weeks. Daisy had the feeling Trent and Rush were glossing over some of the worst parts, and she was glad. When Rush told her about Maria's husband being shot, Daisy gasped, and he quickly added, "But he's making a full recovery. I expect the courage of the man will become as legendary as Maria's and Arizona's own courage. Not only did he make the escape possible, he realized our dilemma in needing his wife to bring June back to Texas and insisted she come with us."

The magnitude of Trent's words brought a contemplative atmosphere to the table. Daisy glanced at the babies sleeping in their cradles in a corner of the room and whispered a silent prayer of blessing over everyone involved in the rescue.

There was one issue, however, not broached during the meal—Elijah Logan—the instigator of the kidnapping. As Daisy lay in bed that night, she asked Tim, "Did Trent mention anything to you about Mr. Logan?"

Turning on his side, he reached to stroke her hair. "Yes. He said the man is still at large."

Daisy whispered in a frightened voice, "What if he tries again?"

Tim smoothed a finger over her lips. "Trent's already initiated extra precautions. The men are on the alert for anything unusual and you and June won't go anywhere without someone accompanying you. And honey," he said with a smile in his voice, "I don't think you realize that Rush was once a bounty hunter. Tomorrow he's riding to town to send wires to several lawmen of reputation who'll get the word out. He and Trent have also posted a generous reward for the man." He leaned over and kissed Daisy's lips. "It's only a matter of time before he's brought to justice."

Encouraged by Tim's words, Daisy lifted a hand to the back of his head, pulling his mouth tightly against hers. "Let's celebrate that good news."

Tim chuckled against her lips, "I love celebrations with you."

Chapter 26: Trent Confesses

Trent never slept past five o'clock, but by the sun's position he knew it was well past that early hour. Physical exhaustion he could deal with, but constant emotional turmoil had taken its toll.

Now that June was restored to her parents, and Maria and her babe settled, the ranch had reverted to some semblance of order. Today, Trent intended to take Arizona aside for a long, heartfelt talk. His deathbed experience, be it real or imagined, had changed his outlook on life. He knew he could now move forward and lay the past to rest—he could find happiness and start a family with Arizona—if she would have him. He hoped his previous bull-headedness hadn't ruined his chances with her.

Sighing, he rolled to the side of the bed and sat up. Running a hand through his hair, he wondered if he looked like hell. Chasing outlaws for weeks and being shot didn't help what he already knew to be a rough countenance.

Pulling a pair of trousers over his long johns, he headed to the indoor water closet to wash up and shave. By the time he entered the kitchen it was already eight o'clock and the hands had long since eaten. He and Rush had ordered all the men to take it easy for a couple of days. Everyone was tired, both the men who had ridden posse and the ones who had stayed behind doing double duty.

Pearl greeted him with a wide grin. "You ready for a mountain of flapjacks?"

He kissed her cheek. "How about half a mountain; my appetite's still coming back. Have you seen Arizona this morning?"

Pearl dumped flour in a bowl. "She left at sunrise with her brothers. Said they'd return the borrowed horses in a few days."

"What!"

Pearl reached for the milk can. "Hmm. Why are you so upset? You been avoidin' that gal fer years."

Trent ignored her question. "Save the flapjacks for later." He strode out of the kitchen, but heard Pearl call, "Well, land's sake, it's 'bout time you got some sense!"

Trent rushed to the barn barely acknowledging morning greetings from his hands, and saddled his horse. Rush entered the barn. "Hey, Trent, what's up? You look like you're on a mission."

Without explanation, he mounted Venus, said, "I am," and galloped toward the main road.

* * *

Arizona had only been home a couple of hours when she heard the sound of hooves pounding up to her soddy. Her heart skipped a beat. Had the rancher who'd ordered the kidnapping found her? Her pa and brothers were away rounding up stray cattle. She rushed to the window and relief washed over her when she saw Trent dismount.

Stepping outside, she frowned at his bleak expression. "Has something bad happened? You look like the grim reaper."

"I need to talk to you."

"Sure. Go ahead."

"Private."

"There's no one home."

"Why the hell did you just take off this morning? Even your pa told you to stay at our place and rest for a few days."

Trent's tone, more than his words, angered Arizona. "In case you haven't noticed, I have a household to take care of. My pa and brothers are terrible housekeepers and, unlike you, I don't have the luxury of hiring help." She inhaled deeply, just winding up. "And who do you think you are to even question me like that. I'm a grown woman and capable of taking care of myself." Suddenly, she blushed. If not for Trent and Rush, she would be dead. She sputtered, "I mean I can take care of myself when I'm not the victim of kidnapping."

She turned on her heel and would have stormed into the house, but Trent caught her by the waist and twirled her around. The action shocked her and she was just about to push him away when she looked up at him.

He was smiling.

"What-what are you doing?"

"Deciding whether I want to kiss you or argue with you."

Arizona's jaw dropped.

Trent said, "I think I'll kiss you."

Her mouth continued to gape, but soon his lips on hers had her returning a kiss that curled her toes. Reaching her arms around Trent's wide shoulders, careful not to put pressure on his wound, she whimpered into his mouth and gave in to years of longing for this stubborn man.

When he broke the kiss and said, "I want to marry you." He had to hold her upright or she would have fallen to the ground.

Before she could respond, he said, "Sit here with me. I need to tell you some things." He motioned to the two rocking chairs on either side of the door.

Arizona practically fell into her chair and Trent positioned his to face her. He covered her hands with his and leaned forward.

Arizona's heart raced.

"Darlin', I want you to know you've always had a place in my heart. When you were a teenager, I admired your spunk, but when you became a woman, my admiration deepened into something more." He glanced down and then returned his sky blue eyes to hers. "I'm sure you've heard the rumors about me and Rush's first wife, Katy." He puffed a breath. "They're true. I loved Katy and compromised her relationship with her husband. When it happened, I discovered that she also loved me. We were in an impossible situation. I had decided to move away, but then she told me she was pregnant. Rush had been away long enough that we knew the baby wasn't his. When he found out, he was livid, but willing to forgive her. He was going to take her away, but she didn't want to leave me.

"One day Rush came into the house and ordered Katy to have Pearl pack her things because they were moving to Laredo so he could buy land and start another ranch. She begged him not to take her away, but he was determined. That night she went into early labor. Pearl was there, but the babe was born dead. Katy died shortly thereafter.

"Rush blamed himself and I blamed myself. He left and didn't return for twenty years, and for twenty years I lived with unspeakable guilt. When he returned and forgave me," his voice cracked, "it was more than I had a right to hope for. But still, guilt plagued me even though my brother and I were restored."

He lifted Arizona's hands to his lips and kissed them. "When I was shot and almost died, something incredible happened. I don't know if it was real or imagined, but I saw Katy."

Arizona gasped and Trent looked concerned. She said, "Oh, Trent, can you tell me about it?"

He smiled. "It's because of Katy that I'm here. I was in a dark tunnel and saw a light that kept getting brighter. I knew Katy was in the light. I asked her if I could stay with her. She said I could, but questioned if I really wanted to. I asked about our baby and she said the child was with her." His voice cracked again. "And they were always with me." Tears sprang to his eyes, but his gaze did not waiver from Arizona's. "Then Katy asked if I really wanted to leave you."

Arizona couldn't breathe.

"I told her you made me feel alive and I wanted to be with you." Again, he lifted and kissed her hands. "After that, I said goodbye and woke to find you next to my bed."

Tears streamed down Arizona's cheeks and Trent released her hands, brushing the tears away with his thumbs. "I love you, Arizona. You make me want things I thought were lost to me. Will you marry me and save me from this wretched loneliness?"

The joy in Arizona's chest erupted and she threw her arms around Trent's neck. "Oh, yes! Yes! Yes!"

Chapter 27: Window to the Soul

Daisy rejoiced when Trent announced to everyone that he and Arizona were to be wed. Arizona had joined them for supper and jovial banter was tossed around the table. Grady sang a little Irish tune he said his father had taught him, and the hands congratulated the happy couple in turn.

Pearl said, "It's about time you two tied the knot. I been tryin' to get ya'll to see the light fer years." Without waiting for a response, she forged on. "I think ya'll should have the weddin' here." She looked steadily at Trent, "Don't you agree?"

Trent grinned. "Pearl, do you honestly think I'm going to contradict what you think?"

The old woman's face crinkled into a smile and her eyes twinkled. "I sure hope not. So…is it okay fer me to plan a feast and celebration right here on the ranch?"

Trent looked at Arizona. "What do you want, honey?"

"I'd love to marry here!"

"Okay, it's settled," Trent confirmed. "Now we need to set a date."

Pearl said, "I needs at least a month to prepare."

Trent frowned. "That long?"

Lilah said, "Don't forget there's a wedding dress to be sewn, so that means a month would be perfect."

Ivy clapped her hands. "I just love pretty dresses. Will you make one for me too, Mama?"

Lilah looked lovingly at her daughter. "I certainly will."

Arizona said shyly to Lilah, "Would it be all right if Ivy is the flower girl in my wedding?"

Ivy squealed. "Oh, Mama, please say yes."

Lilah grinned. "Of course you can be the flower girl."

Trent looked at his brother. With a catch in his voice, he asked, "Would you be my best man?"

With equal emotion, Rush replied, "I would be honored, brother."

Trent looked at Chad. "Son, would you also stand beside me in the wedding?"

The boy, who had been silent until now, said with a wide grin. "Yes, sir. I'd surely like that."

Arizona said, "Well, since you're having a best man, I believe I need some matrons-of-honor." She glanced from Daisy to Maria. "You've both become my dear friends. Would you be my matrons-of-honor?"

Daisy said sincerely, "You have also become my dear friend. I would love to be in your wedding."

Maria gave a timid smile when one of the Mexican hands translated everything that had been said. She replied, "Si. I love to be in wedding."

The table went silent with so much emotion that the hired hands fidgeted. Trent laughed and glanced around. "Men, I thank each and every one of you for your loyalty and hard work and my wedding wouldn't be complete without your presence. We'll make the day a celebration never to be forgotten." He lifted his glass of cider. "To family and friends."

The unease left the table and everyone lifted their glasses. Rush said, "Yes...here's to family and friends."

Daisy lifted her own cider and joined in the toast. The only thing marring such a perfect night was the question as to Mr. Logan's whereabouts and his intent.

* * *

Tim lifted Daisy onto the front of the buckboard, reached for June in Pearl's arms, and then handed the baby to his wife. Next, he helped Pearl into the back and then Maria holding Princesa.

Rush assisted Lilah and his children onto the bed of the other buckboard. He climbed in beside them while Trent hopped onto the driver's seat.

Grady and two other hands mounted their horses to escort the family to town. There had been no sightings of Mr. Logan, but no one was taking chances.

Taking the driver's bench, Tim pushed thoughts of the misguided man from his mind and grinned at the reason for their travel to Harper—his ma and pa, brother and sister, were arriving on the train. He'd written them of his marriage shortly after arriving at Big G and, without going into details, described his joy at becoming June's father. He had also recounted the tornado as being the reason they were in Texas. His ma had written back right away exclaiming her joy and insisting that as soon as they could break away from the farm, she and Cooper and the children would travel to meet Daisy and their new granddaughter. He had not written to them about the kidnapping. That was something that needed to be recounted in person.

Only a week previous, a wire had been delivered giving the time of his loved ones' arrival by train in Harper.

Tim glanced at Daisy and smiled. "I can't wait for you to meet my family."

She looked anxiously at him. "What if they don't think well of me for not being married when I had June?"

Tim reached to place his hand on her knee. "Honey, my family is going to love you and June. Don't you believe anything different. And you're going to love them."

Daisy gave him a tremulous smile.

A few minutes later, Pearl, sitting behind the driver's seat, patted Tim on the shoulder. "Now, Tim and Daisy, I'm gonna tell you my list of items needed for the weddin'. We only gots three weeks to go. When we start back home, if you see I've forgotten anything, you let me know."

"Yes, ma'am," said Tim.

Pearl started listing items.

Tim figured Pearl was trying to keep Daisy from fretting all the way to town and wanted to hug the woman.

Around noon, they entered Harper. The train wasn't scheduled to arrive for another hour so the group decided to eat at a local diner.

It seemed the whole town knew about the return of June, as well as Trent and Arizona's upcoming wedding. Congratulations were being called by everyone who saw them. Inside the diner, their meal was constantly interrupted by well-wishers."

Tim kept glancing at his pocket watch. He couldn't wait to be reunited with his family.

They had just exited the diner when the train's whistle was faintly heard. Daisy clutched his arm. Since there was nothing he could say to ease her nervousness, he bent and leaned his forehead against hers for a second.

The small entourage walked the short distance to the depot as the whistle became stronger and clearer. Finally, the train came into view. A handful of other greeters milled around the landing, but the Big G folks outnumbered them. Finally, the locomotive chugged to a stop and workers rushed to unload luggage from the baggage car and reload the tender for the train's eminent departure.

Tim scanned the windows and spotted his brother Beau waving. His sister Maddie stuck her head next to Beau's and also waved excitedly. He pointed, "Daisy, there's my brother and sister. And there's my ma in the window in front of theirs." His mother grinned and blew them a kiss.

Tim led Daisy closer to the debarking area. The conductor assisted several people from the train and then his ma appeared, followed by Beau and Maddie, and then his stepfather. His mother shouted and Tim ran to throw his arms around her. He hugged her fiercely. She sobbed and laughed at the same time. "I've missed you so much!"

His pa put his arms around both of them and his brother and sister put their arms around their pa.

Cooper said, "It's so good to see you, son."

His mother sniffled and lifted a hankie to her eyes. "I've just got to meet my new daughter."

Cooper released them and Hallie said to Tim. "Introduce us, son."

Daisy had stepped to the side while the family reunited and he walked the few paces to her. With a voice overflowing with pride, he said, "Ma, Pa, Beau, Maddie, I'd like you to meet my wife Daisy and our baby, June." He placed his arm around her and could feel her trembling. To Daisy he said, "Honey, this is my ma, Hallie, my pa, Cooper, and my brother and sister."

Just as Tim had known would happen, his mother wrapped her arms around Daisy. "My sweet girl, it's been years since we parted. Imagine my wonderful surprise when Tim wrote of your marriage." She leaned back and said, "I remember Tim telling me you'd dream of marrying him and how upset he was." She playfully punched her son's arm. "He doesn't look upset now. I can see how happy you've made him." Laughing, she said, "And I must hold my granddaughter, that is, if it's okay with you."

Daisy shyly smiled. "Yes, ma'am. It's perfectly okay." She handed June into her grandmother's loving arms.

While Hallie crooned over June, Cooper gave Daisy a little hug. "I second Hallie's observation that Tim is positively beaming with pride and love."

The affection from Tim's family was obviously easing Daisy's anxiety and she turned to say hello to Beau and Maddie, before receiving June back from Hallie.

Tim's mother glanced past her new daughter-in-law. "Lilah! My sweet sister, you are as beautiful as ever and you look so happy!"

The sisters rushed toward each other and hugged and Lilah said, "I'm *very* happy, and with you being here, I'm fairly bursting."

Hallie reached to hug Rush and then gushed over how much Ivy and Chad had grown in only a year.

Next, she greeted Pearl and the women exchanged heartfelt words.

Neither Maria and Princesa, nor Grady and the two ranch hands that had traveled with them were excluded from the happy greetings.

Tim stood back and watched the family reunion. He said a silent thank you to God that he had followed his heart and returned to Missouri. Daisy was everything he wanted in a wife. She was smart and witty and kind, and lit a fire in his belly that flamed brighter every day.

While he was smiling at the happy scene, he saw a strange expression replace Pearl's happy one and he glanced at the opposite end of the depot. What he saw turned his blood cold. Elijah Logan was striding toward them with a revolver in his hand. Thankfully, it was resting at his side and not pointed at anyone. Rather than shout for everyone to run, Tim stepped away from the group, hoping Rush and Trent would notice. He walked toward the man. He figured he had a good chance of being shot, but at least that would alert everyone to danger.

Mr. Logan hesitated and then continued his pace. At twelve feet, Tim said, "Mr. Logan, you don't want to harm anyone, especially Daisy or your granddaughter."

The man stopped walking and something in his eyes kept Tim talking. "I know what it's like to lose someone you love. My pa died when I was eight. He meant everything to me."

Mr. Logan snarled, "My boy was a bad seed; always in trouble and making foolish decisions. What makes you think I give a heap that he's dead?"

Tim replied softly, "They say the window to the soul is in the eyes. Your eyes reveal your love for Jensen, no matter what he was."

A tortured expression settled on Mr. Logan's face. "I'm a rich man. I could have given the babe and her ma everything. But you got in the way."

Behind Tim, he heard Daisy cry, "Oh, God, no. Mr. Logan, please don't hurt him. I'll do anything…"

Tim shouted, "Daisy, quiet!" He stared Mr. Logan in the eyes. "Yes, you can give them many things, but can you give them this—love, family, happiness. Or will you raise June to become just like her father, a selfish soul without compassion or integrity?" His gaze didn't waiver and neither did Mr. Logan's.

Mr. Logan smiled slightly. "Well spoken." Slowly, he raised his gun. Daisy screamed and a shot rang out. Elijah Logan dropped to the ground and Tim rushed forward. The man was still breathing and stared deeply into Tim's eyes. Tim saw the truth. He said, "You weren't going to shoot me. You wanted to be shot."

With a weak smile, he responded, "Take care of my granddaughter." He closed his eyes and breathed his last.

By now, a crowd had gathered. Tim glanced up to see Grady holding his gun. Grady said, "I hate killin'."

Rush placed a hand on the old man's shoulder. "You did what had to be done. If you hadn't shot him, I would have."

Tim stood and walked toward Daisy standing in the circle of family members. They parted when he reached her. Lifting a hand to her fiery curls, he said, "It's over, darlin'." Bending his knees until his face was even with hers, he smiled, "Let's go home."

Chapter 28: Pins and Pa

Lilah said, "Just a few more pins and you can take the gown off."

Arizona studied herself in the full length mirror in Lilah's sewing room. The dress was exquisite and so much more than she had ever imagined. Between Lilah, Hallie, Daisy, Maria, and Pearl, the women had first sketched and then created a pattern for a dress surely meant for a princess. She wanted to twirl and dance and stay in her wedding dress all day.

Hallie said, "Only two weeks until the wedding, and three weeks until my family returns to Oregon. We're going to miss everyone so much. I wish we could stay longer, but my stepson, Jake, surely has his hands full caring for the farm while we're gone. It was so sweet of him to offer to run things until our return." She glanced at Lilah, "Did I pin this sleeve tight enough?"

"Yes. It's perfect. These alterations should only take a day or two and then we'll do a final fitting."

The women helped Arizona out of her gown and she sighed while fingering the delicate bone-white lace peeking from beneath the rounded neck of the bodice. When Lilah had asked which fabric Arizona wanted her dress to be sewn from, she'd been at a loss to respond. Lilah had merely smiled and pulled fabric bolts until Arizona's face lit. "Oh, I like that one." After that, the dress had emerged into pale blue organdy overlaid with tulle the same color as the lace. Mutton sleeves had been Hallie's idea. Pearl had suggested a cinched waist and wide skirt over generous petticoats to show off Arizona's curves. She'd winked and said, "Trent's gonna be smitten down to his toes when he sees you. He won't know if he's a-comin' or a-goin'." Daisy's suggestion had been to make Lilah's veil of the same tulle. When the dress had finally taken shape, Arizona had exclaimed, "I've never seen anything so beautiful in my life. I can never thank y'all enough for this."

Pearl had hugged her. "Li'l lamb, just seein' how happy you are and how happy you make Trent is all the thanks we need."

Now, with a final sigh, Arizona slipped back into her old gingham day dress. After their engagement, Trent had tried to give her money to buy new clothing, but she'd adamantly refused. Frustrated, he'd said, "You may not accept my gifts now, but after we're married, I'm going to lavish them on you."

As she watched Lilah take the dress to the sewing machine her thoughts turned to her father. Since her return, he had changed. For the past two weeks, she had been staying at Big G at her pa's request. With the help of his sons he was "quitin' the drink," as he put it. He said her bein' kidnapped had made him think long and hard about his sorry-ass self. Over the past week, her brothers had ridden to Big G a couple of times to let her know of their pa's progress, and the last time they'd worn happy smiles.

* * *

The day after Arizona's fitting she rode to her soddy and found her pa hoeing the garden. At her approach, he grinned, lifted his hat to wipe sweat from his eyes, and said, "There's my gal. Whadaya think 'bout yer garden?"

She dismounted and ran to hug the old codger. "I love you, Pa!"

He swiped his face again, but this time it was because of tears. Returning her hug, he whispered, "It shore feels good to work the earth agin."

It was then that Arizona made up her mind to return home to spend the last two weeks before her wedding with her pa and brothers.

As soon as she got back to Big G she went in search of Trent to tell him of her intent.

* * *

Trent left the corral and the filly he'd been exercising. The leather of his chaps and boots couldn't be seen for all the grime. He brushed his sleeves and created a dust cloud. Dirt clung to the sweat on his face.

He saw Arizona walking toward him wearing another old dress and he couldn't wait to shower her with new ones. He'd already tried to do that, but she'd refused. Although it had frustrated him, it had also endeared her to him all the more. She was a woman with high standards; a woman of substance. She was also so desirable he hoped she couldn't see the reaction his body was having.

Leaning against the corral fence, he called out, "Hello darlin'. You look determined to talk to me."

She grinned and his heart melted. When she leaned against the fence also, the horse he'd been exercising stuck her head over the railing and Arizona crooned and patted her.

He waited for her to speak whatever was on her mind.

"I'm going home tomorrow."

He frowned. "There's no need. Your brothers can take care of your pa."

Her eyes wandered over his face in a way that made him want to scoop her into his arms. She said, "In two weeks we'll be married and spending the rest of our lives together. My pa's been a drunkard for years. I'd like to have these two weeks with him. Visiting him yesterday was like going back in time. He was—well—like he was before my ma died."

So much love for Arizona welled up in Trent's heart he disregarded his dusty state and reached to cup the back of her head and bend until his lips lightly grazed hers. "I understand and I'll drive you there in the buckboard myself." He laughed low, "But for now, let's ride out to the ridge overlooking the Nueces. Pearl said her second sight saw us kissing there…and her second sight is never wrong."

Chapter 29: Encountering the Past

Tim drove a wagon filled with his family to Harper. His mother had suggested everyone travel to town for a celebration at the local hotel. On an earlier visit she'd been given a flyer advertising a special night of dining and theater at the fancy *Harper Hotel and Theater.*

Trent, Pearl, Maria, Grady, Rush and his family declined going. Even though they gave reasonable excuses for not attending, Tim suspected they were giving him and Daisy time alone with his family. The wedding was only a week away, and a week after that, his loved ones would be returning to Oregon. Maria's offer to watch June because they were attending the theater was much appreciated. It was with sadness for all that the brave woman's own departure would happen shortly after that of his parents. Rush and another hand were personally escorting her and Princesa back to Mexico. June had taken well to the slow transition to cow's milk and now Maria's return to her husband was eminent.

It was late afternoon when Tim pulled the buckboard in front of the hotel. Of all the buildings in the growing town of Harper, it was the grandest with its red and blue gingerbread trim against pristine white siding. It looked clean and inviting.

Hallie exclaimed, "This is such a lovely building! And the colors are outstanding. I shall describe it to Prudence and Mary. Perhaps they'll want to repaint the orphanage." She added sadly, "Prudence's health has been failing; I hope she doesn't pass while I'm gone. She is one of my dearest friends."

Tim had always loved his mother's compassion and reached to hold her hand. She squeezed his in return and said, "Remember when we were in Westport preparing for our journey to Oregon and you said you were too old to hold your mother's hand? You said only babies did that."

Tim grinned. "I was eight years old and thought I had everything figured out. Now I'll gladly hold my mother's hand."

Hallie said seriously, "I'm going to miss you son, but you've chosen well in marrying Daisy and raising June."

Tim glanced at his wife talking to his stepfather. "I love her, Ma. If I didn't believe in fate before, I do now. Imagine, she dreamed of our marriage all those years ago and it's come to pass."

With a happy heart, Tim led his family into the dining room of the hotel. Their fun-loving conversation was infectious and soon patrons were chatting across their tables with the newcomers and meeting Tim and Daisy. Everyone had heard of the kidnapping and rescue and subsequent confrontation and shooting of the mastermind, and although curious stares were cast at the couple, they were not bombarded for details; folks merely expressed relief that the family had come to no harm.

Expertly, Tim's mother guided conversation away from the incident, but Tim continued his reflection. The wire he had sent regarding Mr. Logan's demise and requesting instruction for disposition of the body had been responded to by the ranch foreman and merely read, BURY HIM THERE.

Returning his thoughts to the conversation around him, he smiled at his little brother's refusal to eat peas and his sister proclaiming how much she loved them. As much as he was going to miss his family, he knew it was time to raise his own children. Almost laughing aloud, he wondered if they would like peas. As for himself, he hated the taste.

After supper, the family walked the boardwalk until dusk and then became the first attendees in line to buy tickets to the theater production of *Life in the Wild West*.

The theater had been constructed adjoining the hotel and boasted the same red, white, and blue color scheme. The red velvets draping the interior walls contrasted with the deep blue velvet of the stage curtain, and gave one the feeling of being in a theater located in a sophisticated metropolis. Tim could almost imagine hackneys, buggies, and every mode of transportation delivering socialites to an evening of theatrical delights.

He laughed at his imaginings.

The family happily found seats near the front and relaxed in red velvet chairs. Curiosity had Tim saying, "I'll join you in a minute. I'd like to look around."

Hallie smiled. "I'm not surprised."

Cooper laughed. "Neither am I. You've always been curious about everything. I remember Captain Jones shooting that snake on the Oregon Trail and cooking it up. When he asked if we wanted to share the meat, your ma politely declined, but you, of course, wanted to try it."

Tim winked. "Years later, I met a drifter who was camped outside of Oregon City and he'd roasted some rattlesnake over his fire. He asked if I wanted some."

Everyone leaned toward Tim and waited for his response. Finally, Daisy said, "Well, what did you say?"

Tim whistled and glanced at the ceiling. His mother chuckled, "Timmy Wells, you answer your wife's question."

With a mischievous hint of a smile, he replied, "It was worse than anything imaginable and I spit it out."

While everyone laughed, he excused himself and walked outside to pace the length of the hotel and theater. While leaning against the siding to contemplate how he could get backstage, two people paused on the boardwalk and he couldn't help but overhear their conversation. In an encouraging voice, a young man said, "Nell, you're going to give the performance of a lifetime. You're the most talented actress I've ever been on stage with."

The woman replied, "And you're the sweetest man I've ever met. But I can't help these feelings. This is my first *big* performance and I just feel so…inadequate. What if I forget my lines?"

The gentleman laughed softly, "Then I'll whisper them to you." In an even quieter voice but still heard by Tim, he said, "I adore you, Nell."

The woman returned his laughter. "I think the reason I was saved by that man during a tornado was just so I could meet you. I feel like we're destined to be together—like we have a purpose. I just…"

"What, honey?"

"I just don't want to disappoint you."

"That will never happen."

Tim frowned. Stepping to the boardwalk, he said, "Excuse me. I wasn't intentionally listening to your conversation, but you said something I must ask you about."

The gentleman slipped his arm around the woman's shoulders in a protective gesture and said hesitantly, "What might that be?"

Tim moved his gaze to the petite woman with a pert nose and curly blond hair upswept under a fashionable hat. "Um, ma'am, you said something about being rescued in a tornado. That wouldn't be the St. Louis tornado of 1866, would it?"

The pretty woman's eyes widened. "Why, yes, it was. There was a man walking across the street and he saw some metal siding coming loose from a building. Although he walked with a limp, he rushed over and threw his body over mine."

Tim knew the answer to his next question, but he asked anyway, "You wouldn't happen to know the man's name, would you?"

I remember that sad day like it was yesterday and the deputy pulling out his wallet and saying his name was Thomas Wells."

Tim croaked, "Ma'am, that man was my father. I'm Tim Wells."

Immediately, tears pooled in the woman's eyes. "I'm so sorry. I've felt guilty all my life that someone died saving me. I wish it had been me so you'd still have your pa."

Tim stepped closer. "Oh, no, please don't think like that. I'm so…so honored to make your acquaintance. I've always wondered what happened to the girl my father saved, and meeting you has given me closure. My father was a wonderful man and he would do it all again."

Tears dripped down the woman's cheeks. "My name is Nell Cavanaugh. May I give you a hug?"

Tim swallowed the lump in his throat. "I'd like that more than anything."

The woman moved away from her companion and reached her arms around Tim's shoulders. In response, he held her lightly, and then tightened his hold. For an instant, it was as if he hugged his father one last time. He stepped back and looked away long enough to wipe a handkerchief across his eyes. In an emotional voice, he said, "My mother is inside. Would you mind if I introduced you to her?"

Nell smiled through tears, "I wouldn't mind at all. Since there's so little time before the show starts, why don't you bring her backstage after the performance?"

Tim glanced at the woman's companion, who smiled. "Yes, bring your mother and whoever else is with you to the side door and we'll leave instructions allowing you to enter."

"Thank you," Tim responded.

The gentleman said, "By the way, my name is Will Tramour and Nell is my fiancée." He placed a hand on Tim's shoulder. "I don't believe I could have written a more profound moment in one of my plays."

No one spoke as the magnitude of the encounter settled into their hearts. Finally, Will turned to Nell. "Honey, we must hurry."

Tim watched them knock on the side door. Immediately, it was opened by a big, brawny man. Returning to his family, Daisy gave him a curious look and his mother leaned toward him. "Tim, something's happened. I can see it in your face."

He patted his mother's hand. "You'll find out soon enough."

Hallie smiled. "Okay, son, I trust you'll let me know when it's time."

Over the next half hour the theater filled to overflowing. Before the production began, Will stepped onstage and proclaimed in a loud, theatrical voice, "I thank everyone for attending. My name is Will Tramour. For many years, I have written plays and traveled the country, but it wasn't until I met Nell Cavanaugh that my plays came alive. Tonight, Nell and our actors are presenting a performance that showcases the perils of westward travel. It is a story overflowing with emotions everyone can relate to, joy and heartache. It is also a story of courage, sacrifice, and discovery. But more importantly, it is about the resilience of the human spirit."

With a flourish of his hands, Mr. Tramour finished with, "And so, without further ado, let the performance begin!" He exited the stage and the curtains opened.

Nell stood alone, center stage, and said in a crisp and beautiful voice, "I know not what awaits me at the end of my journey, but of one thing I am sure—I must journey onward."

For the next hour, the spectators sat riveted by the actors. When a short break was announced, clapping and accolades broke the silence as the curtain closed.

After the break, the audience again became one with the actors. With the final curtain, everyone jumped to their feet in a standing ovation. Nell Cavanaugh and Will Tramour were consummate actors who evoked every emotion. Tim knew his father would be proud.

His brother and sister began rehashing the final scene. Maddie said, "I want to be an actor when I grow up." Beau said, "Me, too!"

Hallie responded, "And so you shall, if that's your heart's desire."

Tim cleared his throat. "Could I have everyone's attention?" His family looked at him expectantly. "When I walked outside earlier, I met two of the actors and they invited us backstage."

Beau whooped with joy and Maddie grinned. Hallie and Daisy both placed their hands over their mouths. Cooper glanced at Hallie. "As you always say on momentous occasions, this is something we'll talk about on long winter nights."

With sincerity, Tim said, "Oh, you have no idea." He glanced at Cooper and asked, "May I speak with you privately for a moment?"

Everyone looked curiously at him. Cooper said, "Of course, son."

Stepping into the aisle and away from his family, Tim spoke low to his stepfather and revealed his discovery. Cooper's eyes widened and he turned so Hallie couldn't see his expression. He said, "Tim, I want you to take your mother backstage alone for this extraordinary meeting."

"Exactly what I was thinking, Pa."

After returning to their family, Cooper touched Hallie's shoulder. "I want you to go first, honey. We'll follow in a few minutes."

Hallie's expression turned curious and then serious. "If you say so."

Tim offered his arm to his mother and led her outside to the stage door. He knocked and the same burley man opened it. "My name is Tim Wells, and this is my mother, Mrs. Hallie Jerome. Miss Cavanaugh is expecting us."

The big man stepped aside. "Yes, she told me. Just follow the hallway to the end and turn left."

Tim did as he was bid. His mother said, "I can't imagine why everyone couldn't go at once, but I trust your reason."

They reached a door that had Miss Cavanaugh's name hanging from it. Tim lightly knocked. Almost immediately, the actress opened her door. With tears in her eyes she said, "Oh, please come in."

Tim ushered his mother inside. Before he could speak, Nell had enfolded her in a hug, sobbing. Hallie reached to comfort the young woman, sending a questioning look at Tim.

Tim's own eyes became moist when he quietly said, "Ma, this is the girl Pa saved in the tornado."

A shocked expression crossed his mother's face and then she gripped the girl in a tight hug. Both women sobbed.

* * *

Snuggled between Daisy and Tim, June slept peacefully. Tim reached to turn out the bedside lamp. The previous evening's emotional meeting at the theater had been recounted to the Big G household and marveled over many times. Tim said, "I believe my life has come full circle and all ghosts have been laid to rest."

Muted light filtered through the draperies and Daisy studied his profile. She reached across June to run a finger down his cheek. "These past months are the stuff of novels. Maybe you should write our story."

He chuckled low and the sound warmed Daisy's heart. He said, "I never told you this, but I write poetry."

Daisy grinned in the dark. "I suspected as much. Perhaps you could put our story into prose."

He laughed. "I wonder what adventures await the rest of our lives. I have a feeling the prose will continue until we draw our last breaths."

"I'd settle for hearing one of your poems now."

"Okay, you asked for it. This one is short and to the point."

Daisy held her breath as Tim said in his deep voice.

*"If not for you,
I would still be seeking that which I have found."*

Daisy's heart radiated love. "That's exactly how I feel."

Tim said, "I wrote it the day after our marriage."

Chapter 30: Crooked Tie

Arizona poured her pa and brothers coffee. Other than a polite thank you from her brothers, no other words were spoken. Glancing at her pa, she said, "I'm going to have my coffee outside. Want to join me?"

"You go ahead."

She looked at her brothers. "How about you?"

Tad shook his head and Slim said, "We got chores."

Arizona kept her face impassive, but hurt stabbed her heart. Since her return two weeks ago, time with her family had been wonderful. Was today different because it was her last day at home? By mid morning they would all be leaving for her wedding in the late afternoon at Big G Ranch. Surely they could spare a few minutes with her.

Her brothers grabbed their cups and headed out the door. She glanced at her pa, but he was staring at the table. Sighing, she stepped outside the soddy that had been her home since she was twelve; the home her mother had died in. Life had changed after her mother's passing. Her pa had turned to drink and she'd had to raise her three brothers. None of them had been able to attend school regularly, but her being the oldest, she'd taught them as best she could.

Walking to the trail that was as familiar to her as the back of her hand, she gulped back tears. Maybe her pa hadn't been the best and her brothers unruly, but she loved them dearly and she supposed, in their own way, they loved her.

Her favorite tree loomed ahead and she veered off the path to sit at its trunk. Squirrels always scampered in the area and she distracted her sadness by watching them dart back and forth.

Closing her eyes she envisioned Trent. He was the finest man she had ever laid eyes on, and the fact that he was in love with her, still amazed her. Shortly after their engagement she'd had second thoughts about their suitability. After all, he was a learned and wealthy land owner, and she, a plain woman raised in a soddy on his land. When she expressed her misgivings, he immediately kissed them away. His kisses always made her breathless and when he asked, "Do you still doubt me?" she'd known in her heart that he loved her deeply.

Arizona sipped the last of her coffee, reflected on her life a few minutes longer and then mentally listed the things still to be accomplished before leaving for Big G. Butterflies knotted her stomach. She was about to go from being a poor farm girl to the wife of the largest rancher in the county—a man of power and influence.

Trying to talk herself out of her jitters, she slowly walked back to her home. When she came within sight of the sod house, she saw her pa sitting in his old rocker outside the front door. He stood when she approached and stepped inside, not even acknowledging her.

Again, an arrow of hurt pierced her heart. Determination came to her rescue and she resolved that her pa and brothers would not ruin the grandest day of her life. She opened the door and entered the soddy. It took a moment for her eyes to adjust to the dim interior, but then her jaw dropped. Standing beside the old cook stove stood her brother, Marty. On the opposite side of the stove Slim and Tad grinned. Her pa waited in the center of the room, a huge smile cracking his weathered face.

Her pa said, "You didn't think we was gonna let our favorite gal get away without a big surprise, did you?"

Tears pooled in Arizona's eyes as she ran and threw her arms around her pa. "Oh, Pa, I'm going to miss you so much!" She turned to hug Marty. "When did you get back? I didn't see your horse."

"I came in the wee hours and stayed in the barn. We wanted to surprise you."

"You've certainly done that. I'm so happy you're here for my wedding." She hugged her other brothers in turn and for the next hour the family sat around their small table catching up on recent happenings, including the kidnapping, and then reminisced old times.

Finally, Slim said, "We best be heading out soon."

Arizona reached to grasp Marty's hand. "You've made this day perfect by returning."

"Big sis, I'm here to stay. Travelin' the country made me realize how much I love home." He glanced at his pa. "I think we can make this ranch much more than what it is. Because of the Garretts' generosity, the land will someday be yours."

Huck responded, "Boys, I think there's plenty of room for more soddys and a passel of grandchildren. Being a drunk for years, I got lots to make up for. I can't turn the clock back on your youth, but I can be a good grandpa."

Arizona's joy was complete when her brothers circled their pa and hugged him. Her pa looked at her. "While the boys hitch up the buckboard and load your trunk, I want to give you somethin'."

Tad, Slim, and Marty left the room and he stepped behind the drape where his bed was. She heard a drawer open and close. He returned with a small box. Arizona already knew what was inside and couldn't swallow for the lump in her throat.

Her pa said, "Honey, here's your ma's wedding ring. I want you to have it and then pass it on to your eldest child. Your ma was the light of my life and I lost my way after she died, but now, with everything that's happened, I feel like I been given another chance. I feel reborn."

Arizona reached for the box and opened it. The simple silver band was more precious than all the gold in the world. Crying unabashedly, she hugged her pa. "This is the happiest day of my life!"

* * *

As usual, Trent couldn't get his string tie to hang straight and made an exasperated sound. Rush had entered his room a few minutes earlier and sat on the bed grinning.

"Not nervous, are you brother?" Rush chuckled.

Trent shot him an anxious look. "Now why should I be nervous when I'm over forty and about to get married for the first time?"

Rush snorted, "If it was anyone but Arizona, you'd have a right to be nervous, but that gal is tailor made for you."

Trent smiled and gave another attempt at tying the string tie. "That she is." He cussed when the tie looked worse than before. "How much time do I have to get this thing from looking like I got my neck cinched in one of Grady's ropes?"

Rush lifted his pocket watch from inside the fancy black vest Lilah had sewn to match Trent's. "Fifteen minutes, give or take a couple." Nonchalantly, he rose and said, "Here let me do it. Lilah taught me how to always make it perfect."

Before Trent could scoff, Rush had his tie looking like he'd stepped off the page of a catalogue. Standing back, Rush perused his brother. "If I do say so myself, my wife's a helluva seamstress. She even made *you* look handsome."

Trent's mouth barely quirked, "Too bad she couldn't do the same for you."

Rush laughed and Trent joined in. He knew all the banter was Rush's way of trying to distract his nervousness. It only worked until there was a knock on the door and Pearl peeked her head in.

"It's time, boys." She laughed and confided, "Guess I should stop callin' ya'll boys, but it ain't gonna happen. You'll always be my boys." A reflective expression passed across her old countenance. "I knows yer pa and ma is here in spirit 'cause I can feel 'em. The day they saved me from the slavers and brought me here has been the joy of my life, but now, seein' both you boys married and happy, this day tops even that." For a long moment she stared from one brother to the other and then quietly closed the door.

The bedroom was silent until Trent said, "I love that woman." Then, "I'm ready, Rush."

Before Trent moved toward the door, Rush grabbed him in a hug. He returned his brother's embrace and silently thanked God and the angelic host that the two of them shared a bond of family and friendship that would never be broken again.

Finally, Rush broke away. "Come on, Trent, let's get you married."

Because Trent had wanted Arizona to have the wedding of her dreams, he had questioned her repeatedly about her desires. As he had already known, she wanted a simple wedding that took place amongst family and close friends. He walked into the living room that had been cleared of furniture and decorated by Pearl, Lilah, Daisy, Hallie, Maddie, Ivy, and Maria. Wild flowers and greenery abounded in vases on the mantle and around the room. His nervousness mellowed and he nodded at those gathered. Close to the big hearth his family and extended family sat in dining chairs moved into the room—Lilah with Chad beside her, Hallie and Cooper, Maddie and Beau, Tim with June standing on his lap and grinning, Pearl seated beside crusty old Grady who was holding Princesa. Across the aisle sat Arizona's father and her brothers, Slim, Tad, and Marty. Trent said with surprise, "Hello, Marty. I'm so happy you're here."

Marty grinned. "Wouldn't have missed it."

The other families leasing land from Big G were in the remaining chairs, while the ranch's hired hands stood off to the side in a gesture of respect for those seated.

Trent walked to stand before Pastor Carpenter in front of the hearth. Rush took his place next to his brother and motioned for Chad to join them. Looking proud and handsome, Chad stepped beside the men. Trent patted him on his shoulder and the boy grinned widely. Mrs. Carpenter began playing a beautiful tune on the piano that had belonged to Trent and Rush's mother. Trent and everyone turned their attention toward the hallway.

Ivy was the first to enter and walk down the aisle tossing colorful rose petals from Pearl's garden onto the ground. Her pretty pink dress highlighted the beautiful coloring she had inherited from her mother. With a look both shy and serious, she performed her task with utmost solemnity, but when she reached Trent, she grinned broadly at him. Everyone sighed at her beautiful smile.

Next, Daisy stepped into the room looking as pretty as a picture in a matching dress. Trent glanced at Tim. The boy was smitten for sure. Unexpectedly, June said, "Mama."

Daisy paused in her progress, got the biggest grin, and blew a kiss toward her baby and husband.

Maria entered behind Daisy and shyly smiled. Her pink dress contrasted beautifully with her Hispanic coloring. She gave a little wave to Princesa who laughed at her mother.

Finally, Mrs. Carpenter changed the tune she was playing and Arizona paused in the entrance. All the air whooshed from Trent's lungs. At one time, he had thought himself only capable of loving Katy, but Arizona had proven him wrong. He loved this courageous, hard-working, shy, funny, and lovely woman with an intensity that made his knees weak. As she walked toward him with tears in her eyes, he figured somehow he'd gotten the second sight Pearl always talked about, because he saw a beautiful future with children and grandchildren, and so much love and happiness his former sorrow was only a memory. In his mind, he heard Katy say, "Trent and Rush, I can now rest in peace knowing you have finally laid the past to rest."

Epilogue

Tired, but strong and healthy, Arizona lay against pillows with her newborn cradled to her breast. She could see that the long night of labor had taken its toll on Trent. As much as she had tried to encourage him throughout the months of her pregnancy, he hadn't been able to completely camouflage his anxiety over his wife having complications.

She now reached to touch his hand that rested against her cheek. "We have a son, Trent."

Tears pooled in his eyes as he moved his hand from her cheek to the baby's. Leaning forward, he kissed his baby and then laid his forehead against Arizona's. "I love you." His breath gently caressed her face and she tilted her head up until her lips touched his. "I know."

After a gentle kiss, she said, "I never told you, but I wouldn't have married Mr. Campbell. I just wanted to make you jealous."

Softly, he kissed her again, "I know, darlin'."

As if aware his parents' attention had been directed away from him, Gus Huckleberry Garrett, named after his grandfathers, let out a loud squall. Arizona laughed against Trent's lips. "I've been waiting my whole life for this."

Research Materials for Daisy: Missouri Challenge

Websites:

freepages.genealogy.rootsweb.ancestry.com/~poindexterfamily/OldWestSlang.html
frisco.org/vb/content.php
literary-liaisons.com/article003.html
tshaonline.org/handbook/online/articles/azr02
tshaonline.org/handbook/online/articles/eqr01
ushist.com/ladies_1800s_clothing/lfhp-materials_ladies.shtml
ushist.com/ladies_1800s_clothing/lfhp-materials_ladies.shtml
Wickipedia.com
wikipedia.org/wiki/St._Louis%E2%80%93San_Francisco_Railway

Author's Note

Many times during the writing of *Missouri Challenge* I found myself close to tears. Revisiting Tim and seeing the sensitive, yet strong and capable man he has become, touched my heart. When Daisy appeared in the story, I marveled at her strength of will in the face of everything she has suffered.

As for Arizona, my hope is that I was able to convey her depth of character, courage, and valiant spirit. Regarding Trent, as soon as he was introduced in book two, *Rescue on the Rio,* my heart broke for him and I knew he had to discover the path leading away from all the loneliness of his life.

Regarding future stories in this series, there are so many characters I could run with—Chad, June, Ivy, Maddie, Jake, Beau, Princesa, Marcus—it's rather mind boggling. Perhaps one of them will whisper in my ear.

My current project is a return to my contemporary western series, *Romance on the Ranch.* After book three, I had decided to end the series, but then characters for book four wouldn't let me be, and *Candy Kisses* was born.

Now, characters for book five have jumped into the limelight, and I must say, I am enjoying the romance between kindhearted socialite, Cecelia Brightman, and world-renown artist, Connor MacKenzie, who lost his wife in a car accident and could possibly lose the use of his right arm if he doesn't have an operation. Little did

Cecelia know that when she missed her footing and toppled on Connor's porch, she was about to meet her favorite artist. I've titled this book *Christmas Kisses* and expect it to be released in time for Christmas, 2013.

For those wanting to read more historical romance, I have included excerpts from all three books in the *Unconventional Series (Abby: Mail Order Bride, Broken Angel, and Ryder's Salvation)*.

Abby: Mail Order Bride (Excerpt) Unconventional Series

Chapter 1: Courage or Folly?

Abigail picked up the newspaper advertisement for the hundredth time, read it again, reread it, and tossed it back on the desk in her library. Smoothing her hand over the sides of her auburn hair and the bun at the nape of her neck, she pushed her chair back and walked from the library to the parlor. Pacing the length of the lovely room, she stopped occasionally to straighten a vase or lift a family photo, all the while contemplating something so crazy it made her heart pound.

After an hour, she squared her shoulders, returned to the library, sat at her desk, slipped a piece of stationary from the drawer, reached for her ink and quill, and wrote:

March 18, 1886

Dear Mr. Samson,
I am writing to introduce myself. My name is Abigail Mary Vaughn and I read your classified advertisement in the Philadelphia Inquirer seeking a wife to help raise your three children. I would like to recommend myself. By trade, I am a teacher and that would benefit your children.

I have never been married and I am thirty-eight years old. I have lived in Philadelphia all my life and taught school for the past eighteen years. I am an only child and my parents died last year so there are no responsibilities keeping me here. I have always desired my own family, but circumstances of caring for my elderly parents prevented that.

I do not believe in withholding information, so I have been candid in my response to you. I hope to hear from you.

—Miss Abigail Mary Vaughn

Before she could react and change her mind, Abigail enclosed the letter in an envelope and asked Harry Puffins, her old servant, to walk it to the post office not far from her home near the city's center.

* * *

Brant removed his cowboy hat and ran a hand through hair as black as coal. Standing in front of the blacksmith's where he'd just had his horse shod, he heard his daughter calling from the entrance to Clyde Jenkins General Store across the street. Clyde, being the most likely candidate, was also the postmaster for the central eastern Texas town of Two Rivers. Jenny held her baby brother in one arm and waved letters in the other. "Hey Pa, you got more mail. Maybe you'll find us a Ma in this bunch."

Brant paused while a buckboard pulled by a swayback horse ambled past. He waved at old Mr. and Mrs. Snodgrass and then crossed to the warped boardwalk that ran in front of a dozen businesses.

"Jenny, did you give Mr. Jenkins that list of staples so we can pick them up next trip to town?"

"Yes, sir." She shifted two year old Ty to her other hip. "One of the letters came all the way from Philadelphia."

"I'll read them tonight. Where's Luke?"

"He's still talking to Mr. Jenkins about ordering some more dime novels."

Brant bent and kissed his baby's forehead. "Well, run in and tell him it's time to go while I hitch Sugar back to the buckboard and bring it around. We've got chores to finish up."

"Sure, Pa."

Several minutes after Brant had pulled the wagon in front of the store, his fourteen year old son sauntered out. Inhaling a calming breath, he said, "It's nice you could join us, Luke. I'd sure like to get home before nightfall. If not, you'll be mucking the barn in the dark."

With a sullen look, Luke hopped onto the back of the wagon and sat on a sack of grain. Jenny snickered and Ty scrambled to sit on his big brother's lap. Brant flicked the reins. "Giddy-up."

After a long evening of chores, Brant finally collapsed into his favorite chair and propped his feet on the hearth. He could hear Jenny telling Ty a bedtime story in the room she shared with her baby brother. No doubt Luke was in the loft devouring another cheap novel.

Leaning his head back, he surveyed his cabin. Besides his bedroom and Jenny's room, there was an additional bedroom that his mail order bride would stay in until they got to know each other. His plan to remarry scared the bejesus out of him, but he was dead set to find a ma for his children. He closed his eyes and saw Molly's laughing face. God, he missed her. How he'd loved her. His eyes stung and he blinked rapidly, glancing again around the combined living, dining, and cooking area that still held her touches in the curtains and knickknacks. Although modest, the cabin was sturdily built from the labor of his own hands.

Unable to put it off any longer, he unfolded his lanky frame and reached for the letters he'd tossed on the mantel. Sighing, he read more responses to his advertisement, none of which he felt any inkling to respond to. Damn, but the thought of marrying someone he'd come to know through a newspaper ad irked him. However, his children needed a mother. Jenny did the best she could caring for Ty, but she was only ten years old. Guilt plagued him at the responsibility that had been forced on her. As for Luke, Brant hadn't been able to bond with his son since Molly's death, and now the boy lost himself in dime novels. And Ty, his baby, God help him, needed a mother's care.

He fingered the letter from Philadelphia. He'd placed ads in newspapers, local and cross country, and wondered if the call of the West would provoke responses from city girls. He'd received a few, but from the tone of their letters, they'd seemed too high and mighty to live in a humble cabin on a small ranch. He slipped a thumb under the envelope flap and ripped it open. The letter was short and written on quality stationary in neat printing. He read it a couple of times.

Going to his room, he retrieved a paper and his quill and ink and brought the kerosene lamp to the dining table. Tapping his jaw, he thought about his response.

May 1, 1886

Dear Miss Vaughn,
Thank you for your letter and also your forthrightness. Please tell me more about yourself and why you would want to marry someone you have never met and mother children that are not your own.
As for myself, I will also be forthcoming. I am solely seeking a mother for my children. If you have romantic notions, I am not the husband for you. My wife died over a year ago from lung fever. I have two sons, a fourteen year old and a two year old, and a ten year old daughter. My ranch is small, as is my cabin, so if you are looking for anything else, I suggest you not respond to this letter.
As for your qualifications, they are excellent. My eldest son loves reading. I can hardly get him to complete his chores without a book in hand. My daughter is very smart and an avid learner. Both children attended school until their mother died. My eldest son now helps me on the ranch and my daughter cares for her baby brother. My desire is for them to return to school after I marry. I am the son of a teacher so I know the importance of education.

As for Two Rivers, it is a small town that does not have much in the way of diversion to keep folks interested.

So, as you can see, I have not painted a pretty picture. I have written the truth so as not to waste your time or mine.

—Brant Samson

Broken Angel (Excerpt)
Unconventional Series

Chapter One: Angel in Need

Luke Samson followed the waiter in the expensive restaurant to a tiny table for one. After a month's visit with his family in Two Rivers, a small town south of Dallas, he was ready to kick back and enjoy a steak dinner with all the trimmings. Although his stepmother had fed him well, no one prepared steaks like Porter's Steak and Ale. Every time he was in Dallas he ate at the popular restaurant.

Dimly lit by gas lamps, a certain mysterious charm hovered over the tables and patrons. Making himself comfortable at his corner table, he stretched his long frame, thinking about the next installment of the series he was writing. His stories were in demand and he grinned, remembering how his beloved stepmother had asked him at the age of fourteen to enter a writing contest sponsored by the Philadelphia Inquirer. He had balked at her request but his father had insisted he enter. To his amazement, he had won the contest and shortly thereafter been asked to write serializations. Over the years, popularity for his adventure tales had increased and his stories were widely circulated. Generally, he wrote a twenty-part series that was eventually published in book collections of five stories each. Now, at the youthful age of twenty-five, he had amassed a small fortune.

His waiter returned with a mug of ale and he placed his order: steak—rare, baked potato and hot bread, both dripping with butter, green beans, salad, and a large slice of his favorite dessert, apple pie.

Settling back again, he closed his eyes and smiled, reminiscing his visit with his family. His father, as strong and active as ever, still behaved like a lovesick schoolboy around Abby, his stepmother for over ten years now. His brothers, nine year old James and seven year old Rusty, had him chuckling aloud. Had he, himself, been that mischievous?

The only person he hadn't seen during his visit was his sister, Jenny. Now twenty-one, she had refused to marry any of the suitors who had come courting, instead choosing to travel to New York to study art at a respected academy. When his father had shown him Jenny's latest paintings, he had stood riveted by her portrayals of country scenes that always made him feel as if he could step into them.

Taking another sip of ale, he switched his thoughts to a classified advertisement he had read that morning in the *Dallas Morning News* and shook his head. Never had he read anything so blatant.

Mrs. Angel St. Clair, a widow, is seeking a husband to accompany her to California. Said husband will be paid handsomely for the escort and then released from matrimony after safely depositing Mrs. St. Clair at her destination.

Luke shook his head. The woman must be desperate to have to advertise for a husband, and the fact that it would end in divorce, simply boggled his mind. The posting made no sense.

Absentmindedly, he heard chairs scraping and patrons being seated behind him. He paid little attention until he heard a gentleman say, "Now, Mrs. St. Clair, may I call you Angel?"

A woman with a voice as smooth as aged brandy said, "Mr. Pinkle, I do not seek to offend you, but I would prefer being called Mrs. St. Clair, for the time being, at least."

The gentleman sounded slightly offended when he responded in his nasally voice. "Of course, as you wish." He continued, "Now as I was saying at our previous dinner engagement, I believe I am the perfect husband to protect you on your journey to California. I have traveled there before and I am aware of the perils that could befall a woman traveling alone. I would protect you with my life."

Luke listened to the exchange in fascination and finally, not caring that it would appear rude, turned to look at the woman who had become infamous in his mind. At the same time a waiter stepped between their tables.

Damn!

Rather than turn back around, he waited for the attendant to set water glasses down and leave. For reasons unknown, his heart pounded. Finally, the waiter stepped aside.

And then he saw her.

Ryder's Salvation (Excerpt)
Unconventional Series

Chapter One: Saying Goodbye

Leaning against the hard cushion of the stagecoach, Jenny closed her eyes and sighed. The travel time from Two Rivers to Bingham was three hours, and then she had a two hour wait until her train left for Dallas. The coach hit a rut and she groaned when she bounced several inches off her seat. Opening her eyes, she noticed her traveling companions, a full-figured, red-headed saloon type gal, and a handsome blonde man with matching mustache and goatee, didn't even flinch at the jostling of the coach. The pretty woman whose features had been enhanced by rouge and the darkening of her eyelids, smiled in a friendly manner and said as if she had read Jenny's mind, "Joe and I been traveling the country for eleven years and I think we've hit every rut in every road. The ruts in this one are nothing compared to the ones in Tennessee. Don't you agree, Joe?"

Joe barely slit his eyes open. "No, the ones in Arkansas are worse."

The lively woman laughed, "You know, come to think of it, you're right." She looked back at Jenny. "By the way, my name is Priscilla Clarkson, but my stage name is Princess Prisca."

Jenny grinned at the woman. "My name is Jenny Samson. I'm pleased to meet you."

"Likewise. And that man who's about to start snoring is Joseph Stillwater."

Without opening his eyes, Joseph stifled a yawn and said, "Pleased to me ya, Jenny. Just call me Joe."

"Umm, pleased to meet you, too."

Priscilla said, "So, Jenny, have you ever been to a theatrical performance in a saloon?"

Taken by surprise at her question, Jenny replied, "No. No ma'am."

Priscilla laughed so hard she snorted. "I can't remember the last time I was called ma'am in such a respectful way. Jenny, you just call me Prisca, like all my friends. Do your friends call you Jen?"

"My family doesn't, but some of my friends in New York do."

"New York! Are you traveling all the way there?"

"Yes. I've been visiting my family for a couple of months, but I'm returning to art school in New York. I have another year before I graduate."

"That sounds interesting. What are they teaching you?"

"I'm learning to paint with both oils and water colors, but oils are my favorite."

"My ma could draw pretty good and she tried to teach me, but I never got the hang of it. I was always wantin' to sing anyway. What do you paint?"

"Mostly landscapes or country scenes—lakes, mountains, meadows, cabins, barns—that sort of thing."

"Do you paint people?"

"I have. But not often. I'm going to paint my niece, though. She was born shortly after I arrived for my visit and she's the most beautiful baby I've ever seen. Of course, between her mother's beauty and my handsome brother, how could she not be?"

"Sounds like you have a wonderful family."

"I do. My pa remarried after my ma died when I was nine and my stepmother was a godsend. Her and my pa had two boys, so I have three brothers."

"I had an older brother, but he died when I was seven. My ma and pa wanted more kids, but they was never blessed with them. My pa died when I was sixteen; my ma not long after that. I was left to fend for myself and that's when Joe came along." Prisca glanced fondly at him. "He taught me how to sing in front of people and we've been traveling together ever since."

Jenny glanced at Joe and he made a snoring sound.

Prisca laughed. "Yep, he can sleep through anything."

Jenny asked, "At the risk of sounding nosey, where is your next…er…theatrical performance?"

"We're headed to Bingham for a week, then on to Dallas and Ft. Worth for a month and then to Shreveport for two weeks. After that, we got some performances lined up in Baton Rouge. And after that, don't know. That's the way this business is—up and down."

The remainder of the journey was delightful with Prisca's lively personality and generous smiles endearing her to Jenny. Jenny knew that "proper" women would look down their noses at Prisca, but she found her charming.

After Joe woke, he joined their animated conversation and helped pass the hours. Jenny couldn't help but notice that the same glances she often saw pass between Luke and Angel, also passed between Prisca and Joe—like they shared a secret known only to the two of them. She also noted that Prisca often touched Joe and he responded with smiles and return touches. She wondered if they were married, but remembered Prisca had introduced them with different last names. Their relationship intrigued Jenny, but, of course, she did not pursue her curiosity with questions.

Ahead of schedule they rolled into Bingham laughing at one of Joe's stories. Prisca swiped tears from her eyes. "Every time he tells that calamity I can't stop laughing."

Jenny replied, "That is one of the funniest misadventures I've ever heard," and dabbed tears of mirth from her own eyes.

Jenny was sad to bid Prisca and Joe goodbye and made them promise to look her up if their travels took them to New York in the next year or back to Two Rivers after that.

After disembarking, the stagecoach driver loaded Jenny and her suitcase onto a buckboard bound for the train depot. At the depot she bought her ticket, sat on a bench, pulled a small book of poetry from her reticule, and prepared to wait two hours for her departure. After an hour, thirst and hunger led her inside. Finding a table in a small dining room, she ordered a glass of milk and a slice of apple pie. With her first bite she realized it was nowhere near as delicious as her sister-in-law's.

Angel's baking skills had garnered her quite a reputation in Two Rivers and the surrounding areas. In fact, the Mayflower Hotel dining room was always booked on the weekends with folks wanting to enjoy the meals prepared by Jack and Bessie Jane Smythe and the desserts by Angel.

Settling back in her chair she passed the time by thinking about her family. Several months previous, she had received a letter from her stepmother that her father had been badly injured, but the letter had been sent when he was well on the road to recovery. Abby had apologized for waiting so long to inform her, but she had said that if she'd written sooner, she knew Jenny would have dropped everything to return home. Ma Abby had been right about that. The only thing more important to Jenny than her artwork was her family.

Abby's letter had also contained the news of Luke's marriage and a baby expected about the time of the family's annual trek to the graves of Jenny's birth mother and baby brother. Enclosed with Abby's letter had been a letter from Luke with a bank draft for enough money to buy her passage to Two Rivers during spring break.

Now that her visit was over, Jenny was excited to return to her studies, but sad to leave her family. Her father had completely recovered, and, except for the ragged line of a scar down his cheek and a slight limp, he was back to ranching and raising his family.

Jenny chuckled softly when she remembered walking into the barn during her visit and surprising her pa and ma lying in a mound of hay and kissing passionately. They had both jumped to their feet and Abby had turned swiftly around to rearrange her clothing while Jenny had merely laughed, and said, "Pa and Ma, if you only knew how many times I walked into the barn and saw the two of you kissing while I was growing up, you'd be right embarrassed."

About that time, Jenny's younger brothers, eight year old Rusty and ten year old James, had entered the barn and Rusty had said, "James, it's just Ma and Pa playing in the hay again."

Jenny stifled a loud laugh at her memories and finished her pie and milk. Returning to the depot landing her thoughts turned to her studies at *Jake Ryder's Academy of Art* in New York. She had one month to finish and prepare for a showing of two of her best paintings. Each summer, the academy selected twenty students to showcase their artwork at a popular downtown gallery. The event was attended by both critics and the public and had launched the careers of several students over the years. Just thinking about the showing tied Jenny's stomach up in knots. It was rumored that maybe the great painter and founder of the academy, Jake Ryder, himself, would attend this year. Of course, he hadn't been seen at the last two showings, so her expectation was low that he would appear at this one. Still, one could always hope. Jenny wanted desperately to meet the Painter of Emotions as he was known in the echelons of the art world. Often, since coming to New York, she had stood before his masterpieces that hung at the academy, and even visited the museum that housed some of his most famous works, and gazed in awe at the depictions of Wild West scenes. His mastery of capturing the spirit of whatever he painted mesmerized her. She could stand riveted for long periods viewing every detail of the sky, plains, grasses, mountains, forests, horses, cabins, teepees, cowboys, Native Americans, or whatever was depicted, and her heartbeat would quicken. She always left the presence of his art wanting to cry because he no longer painted. She had read in a Bingham newspaper a few years back that a carriage accident had led to the amputation of his right arm just below his shoulder. Although the article had been unclear as to the exact nature of what had happened, it had quoted Mr. Ryder as saying he could no longer paint because he was right-handed. With an understanding of the devastation he must be feeling because of her own passion for painting, Jenny had cried for him. When she had been accepted into his academy, her sorrow for Mr. Ryder had only intensified.

"Now boarding for Dallas!" yelled the steward.

Jenny mentally shook thoughts of Jake Ryder from her mind. She would probably never meet him, so it was best not to dwell on the sad events of his life.

Novels by Verna Clay

Western Romance

Contemporary:
Romance on the Ranch Series
Dream Kisses
Honey Kisses
Baby Kisses
Candy Kisses
Christmas Kisses

Historic:
Unconventional Series
Abby: Mail Order Bride
Broken Angel
Ryder's Salvation

Finding Home Series
Cry of the West: Hallie
Rescue on the Rio: Lilah
Missouri Challenge: Daisy

Fantasy Romance

Shapeling Trilogy
Roth: Book One: Protector
Fawn: Book Two: Master
Davide: Book Three: Prince

11:11: Countdown to 2012

The Theory of Everything

Made in the USA
Charleston, SC
20 November 2013